WAHIDA CLARK PRESENTS

VINDICATED LOVE

BY

TASHA MACKLIN

D1198355

Wahida Clark Presents Publishing
60 Evergreen Place
Suite 904A
East Orange, New Jersey 07018
973-678-9982
www.wclarkpublishing.com

Library of Congress Cataloging-In-Publication Data:
Vindicated/ by Tasha Macklin
ISBN 13-digit   978-1936649-33-4 (paper)
ISBN 10-digit   1936649330 (paper)
ISBN 978-1-936649-58-7 (e-book)
LCCN 2012913335

1.   Fiction 2. Brooklyn, NY   3. Drug Trafficking-   4. African American-Fiction-   5. Urban Fiction   6.thug life

Cover design and layout by Nuance Art, LLC
Book design by NuanceArt@aCreativeNuance.com
Edited by Linda Wilson
Proofreader Rosalind Hamilton

Printed in USA

Prologue

I think Mel and Alex are having an affair." The statement hung in the air like a mist, slowly seeping into the room until it was filled with tension.

Santiago looked at Basim calmly but intently. "What . . . did you say?"

Basim took a deep breath. He knew when it came to Santiago's wife, he had to tread lightly. Mel was Santiago's heart, a woman Santiago would die for . . . kill for.

"Look Santiago, you know I wouldn't be coming at you like this unless I was absolutely sure. You are like—naw, fuck that—you *are* a brother to me, and I know how much you love Mel."

Santiago shook his head as he paced the room, drink in hand. His heart refused to believe what his head told him was true. Basim was his closest friend, his third in command, a man he would entrust his life to. Still, it didn't make his words any easier to hear.

"What makes you think that?" Santiago asked. He downed his drink and reached for the Hennessy bottle.

"Relax, Big Brah, you know you don't take alcohol well," Basim reminded him.

"Just answer my fuckin' question!" Santiago growled, wanting the warm feeling to engulf him before he did something stupid.

Basim sighed, then replied, "All right . . . you know Renee, right? The bitch I'm fuckin', owns the salon downtown?"

"What about her?"

"She's also a stylist for the chick that does Mel's hair."

"Small world," Santiago quipped bitterly.

"Indeed . . . Anyway, Renee told me she was at the other chick's salon, the one Mel goes to, and Mel was there. Now, she knows Mel, but Mel doesn't know she knows me. Renee said Mel was outside talking to a Spanish looking dude in a yellow Maserati," Basim explained.

"Alex!" Santiago hissed.

Basim nodded grimly. "Who else pushes a yellow Mas' in the city? She said she really didn't pay attention until Mel leaned in and gave him a kiss and he slapped her on the ass."

Santiago squeezed the glass in his hand. If it had been any thinner, it would have shattered in his hand. The thought of another man's hand on his wife's ass had him on fire. "Go on."

"When she told me, I'm thinkin', This bitch trippin'. Ain't no way Mel would play you like that. Broad daylight? Fuck no, but then . . . I saw it for my own eyes . . . I figured maybe if she did it once, she'd do it again, you know? So, the next time she got her hair done I followed her," Basim said.

Santiago eyed him hard. "You what?"

"I foll—"

Santiago shot to his feet and got in Basim's face so close, Basim could smell the liquor on his breath.

"Big Brah, be easy. Let me explain."

"Why the fuck didn't you tell me? It wasn't your place to follow my goddamn wife!" Santiago bassed.

Basim nodded, absorbing his anger. It wasn't that he was scared, being he was 6-feet 4-inches tall and outweighed Santiago by fifty something pounds, but he knew he had to speak carefully concerning Mel.

"Santiago, I know you. I would've never come to you with that if I was unsure, because for one, you would've went off, and if anything was goin' on, you would've only made speculation worse. Now we know for sure."

The two men eyed each other. Finally, Santiago broke the tense silence.

"What did you see?"

"I saw what Renee saw . . . minus the kiss and the slap. But she was definitely talking to Alex," Basim replied.

Santiago refilled his glass while his mind tried to wrap itself around his new reality. Up to that moment, he had been the master of his own destiny, now it seemed that destiny was mastering him.

In every sense of the word, Santiago Acevedo was a boss. Men respected and feared him, and women worshipped and desired him. He held a striking resemblance to the actor Alex Rodriguez, but that is where the similarities stopped. Unlike the actor, everything was real with Santiago. He may have looked like a pretty boy, but he was a stone cold killer at heart. He ran his empire with an iron fist in a velvet glove. Basim was his top lieutenant, overseeing all street business across the city. His cousin Alex was his right hand man. His son Tariq, although only seventeen, was shaping up to be the ruthless image of his father. But when it came to Santiago's heart, his wife Mel and daughter Eva were the center of his world. He may've had a chick or two on the side (what man doesn't), but Mel was his queen and he treated her as such. To hear that she was stepping out on him, and with his own blood, the thought alone had his whole head fucked up. He wanted the Hennessy to drown it away.

He threw his head back and downed his glass.

"Big Brah . . ." Basim said, almost pleading.

"I'd rather be drinking blood," Santiago spat, wiping his mouth with the back of his hand. The liquor was beginning to take effect.

"And there's more," Basim reluctantly added.

Santiago chuckled drunkenly. "There always is."

He didn't know how right he was.

"Did you know Alex's set up down South?"

"Yeah. I gave him the green light."

"Yeah, well, word is Alex and them been buying a lot of guns, stocking up, which can only mean one thing," Basim stated grimly.

"War," Santiago replied, finishing Basim's thought.

Basim nodded. "Exactly. I've been tellin' you for a while that Alex wanna be you. Now, it looks like he's makin' his move."

Santiago couldn't deny the veracity of Basim's words. Alex had always wanted what Santiago had, patterning himself after Santiago's mold. Now it seemed the student wanted to test the teacher, but the teacher was more than ready.

Basim looked at Santiago. "What do you want me to do?"

Santiago poured another drink, then stumbled over to the deep, plush leather armchair and slumped in it, spilling all the liquor in the process.

"Nothing," he replied, taking a sip. "Yet, I'm not doubting, but I need to be sure. Once I am . . . then I'll take care of it," Santiago said. The look in his eyes said it all.

Basim nodded, downed his drink and stood up. "I feel you. But you already know, if you need me . . ."

Santiago mustered a smile. "I already know, Lil Brah. I already know."

Basim turned for the door.

"Why is it always family, Bas?" Santiago asked. The tone of his voice caught Basim in his feelings.

Without turning back, Basim answered, "Because they're the only ones close enough to hurt you." Then he walked out.

Santiago rested his spinning head against the plushness of the green armchair, feeling nuzzled even though he was drowning in confusion.

Mel . . . he thought.

Her beautiful brown face floated before his eyes, and that smile of hers, the one that used to warm his heart seemingly mocked him in laughter. He put his fists to his eyes, but he couldn't erase her image being beamed straight from his heart. All of a sudden, he flung his half empty glass against the heavy oak wall, shattering the glass and watching the liquid streak the wall.

"Bitch!" he spat.

His thoughts wandered . . . stumbled . . . fell back, back into time and how it all began . . .

Chapter 1

Money, Power, Respect

(Santiago's Story)

Twenty years earlier ...

O ohhh, fuck me, daddy, real gooood," the big breasted Cuban said in Spanish as Carlos pounded her pussy, doggy style. Her big, juicy breasts swung with every thrust of Carlo's dick, making her howl with pleasure.

"What she say! What she say!" a thirteen-year-old Basim questioned in a feverish whisper.

Santiago, Basim, and Alex stood on their tippy toes on top of a trash can peeping into the bedroom window and doing a bad job of being sneaky. Darkness served as their cover as the moon cast three eager, sexually-charged shadows on the grass beneath them. Yet, the light inside the huge room provided a drive-in movie view for the perfect summer evening.

"She said—" a twelve-year-old, wide-eyed Alex started to translate, but Santiago cut him off.

"Shhhh! They gonna hear us! Cállate!" he spat with authority. Being that he was the eldest at fifteen, he was the leader of his crew.

All three boys turned their attention back to Carlos and the woman. Even from outside they could hear how wet her pussy was. Every stroke smacked off as if kissing the air. Carlos slid two fingers in her ass and made her grip the sheets with her fists.

"Oh yes, daddy! Fuck my tight asshole! Put the big dick in my ass!"

With a grunt, Carlos pulled his dick out of her pussy and slid it in her ass. Her puckered hole opened up to his girth making her buck back against him.

"Take this dick, puta!"

"I'm your puta, baby. Fuck me!" she squealed.

"What's puta mean?" Basim questioned, his young boy dick tenting his jeans.

"Bitch," Santiago answered.

He was just as hard as Basim and stuck on the fuck faces the Cuban woman was making. He was stuck on the way she bit down on her bottom lip, the way her lips formed sensual O's every time Carlos hit the right spot.

Suddenly, Alex, trying to inch forward on his trash can, teetered and lost his balance. "Oh shit!" he cursed, reaching out to grab at Santiago's arm, but instead of gaining his balance, he up ended Santiago too.

Alex flew backward, taking Santiago with him. In the process, Santiago's trash can hit Basim's, and he too came tumbling down. As the three young peeping toms tried to extricate themselves from the scattered trash and each other, two gunshots rang out.

Pop! Pop!

The three of them looked at each other, wide-eyed and nervous. Forgetting they were covered in trash, they scampered to their feet and tried to run off. They ran right into a naked Carlos, gun in hand and aimed right at them.

"Pop, it's us!" Alex blurted out, blood curdling in his veins.

Looking down the barrel of death, all three of them froze.

"Fuck!" Carlos spat angrily, looked at them and spat again, "Fuck! What the hell were you doing?"

They all looked from one to the other, not wanting to be the one who spilled the beans. Out of the blue, Carlos burst out laughing.

"You lil' fuckin' perverts. You were watching me, weren't you?" He laughed, seeing the three trash cans overturned. He laughed harder, then abruptly stopped. "Do you know what you have fuckin' done? Huh?

Digame!" Carlos roared, putting the fear of God in the three young boys.

Santiago knew his uncle wasn't called El Loco for nothing, because he was truly crazy and he looked it. Carlos looked like the Mexican actor, Danny Trejo from the movie *Machete*. His harsh, leathery face was always in a scowl, and Mexican tattoos worshiping the devil and celebrating Santeria covered his muscular body. But standing there butt naked and armed, Santiago didn't know what to expect. Especially since he still didn't know where the gunshots had come from.

"We're sorry, Papi," Alex said with his head bowed.

"No, you are not sorry yet. But you will be," Carlos replied, giving them a maniacal grin! "Come on!"

The three of them fell in step behind him. They followed him to the bedroom. When they walked in, all of their eyes almost popped from their head. On the bed, the Cuban woman was sprawled out, or what was left of her was. She lay face down, and the back of her head was blown out. Bits of brain, blood, and hair stuck to the wall and head board. The boys couldn't believe their eyes.

When Carlos heard the trash cans crash against pavement, he thought the Cuban woman had brought robbers there to set him up. He didn't hesitate. He grabbed his chrome .45 from under the pillow and blasted two shots into the back of her head. The only mercy was she never saw it coming.

"I thought the bitch was trying to set me up." He laughed, reading Santiago's quizzical expression, then he shrugged. "Oh well, never trust a woman, eh?" He went to put on his pants and shoes while the boys stood transfixed. They couldn't take their eyes off the body. Once Carlos was dressed, he turned to them, smiled and said, "This is your fault, so you are going to clean it up. Grab that sheet."

Santiago's arms hurt so bad they burned. He felt like he couldn't lift them another inch. But whenever he stopped, Carlos would say, "Keep digging."

Basim and Alex's arms felt the same way. They were deep in a wooded area on the other edge of Brooklyn. They had been digging all night it seemed. It took them close to six hours, but just when they felt they couldn't possibly dig another inch, Carlos finally said, "That's deep enough."

The hole was deep enough that they were in it past their waists. The whole time they were digging, Carlos sat on the hood of the car smoking Marlboros.

"Papi, estoy cansado," Alex whined.

Carlos snorted. "You should've thought of being tired when you were in my fucking window. Ven aqui!" He walked to the trunk of the car, with the three of them right behind him. When he opened the trunk, the stench of the rotting body hit them full in the face so hard, Basim threw up.

"Bury that, too," Carlos growled at Basim, pointing at the vomit. Then he turned to Santiago. "Grab her feet."

He and Carlos lifted the body from the trunk. Her skin felt clammy and clay-like in Santiago's hand. He could tell she was dead.

They carried the body over to the hole and dumped it in. When it hit bottom, it rolled over on its stomach, giving them a full view of her voluptuous ass.

"What a waste," Carlos remarked, shaking his head.

Santiago looked down at the body for a minute, then he looked up at Carlos and asked, "What does it feel like to kill somebody?"

Carlos knew right then that Santiago had the stomach for murder. It was the look in his eyes and his total lack of concern for the deceased. He simply wanted to feel it. Carlos smiled and replied, "It makes you feel like God."

Santiago nodded and looked back down at the body while Carlos went back to the trunk. He returned with a white plastic bucket.

"Que es eso?" Santiago questioned.

"It's time. You sprinkle it over the body and in a few days, no more body," Carlos explained, wiping his hands in a gesture to emphasize his point.

Santiago helped him sprinkle the Lyme. When they were finished and the body was buried, Santiago turned and said, "Uncle Carlos . . . I want to be like you."

The comment caught Carlos off guard, but he had half expected it. All the signs had been there for months now. Burying the body had become his confirmation, like a rite of passage. He looked from Santiago to Basim, to his own son, Alex. Basim and Alex returned his gaze and nodded. He knew they would walk in his footsteps, because whenever Santiago led, they followed.

Carlos lit another Marlboro, stroked the stubble on his chin, then asked, "Why? Why do you want to be like me?"

"Money," Santiago replied, "I want to be the richest man in the world."

Carlos looked at Basim.

"Power," Basim replied. "Men fear you."

Carlos looked at his son. "Why mi nino?"

"Power," Alex answered firmly.

Carlos shook his head at them all. "No. If you do it, do it to be respected as men. To prove you are worthy of the air you breathe. A lazy man is worse than a woman. He deserves to be treated as such. But men"—He banged his fist on his barrel chest to make his point— "We are respected, tu entiendes?"

Santiago nodded.

"Yes . . . I understand."

"Then come. You have much to learn."

Chapter 2

Blinded

Present Day

The sounds of 2 Chainz boomed through the strip club, as Tariq and his entourage played VIP getting Don–type attention. All eyes were on his eight-man team as the bubbly flowed and the bitches stayed just as wet.

Tariq snorted a thick line of coke from the black marble table, then shook his head, pinching and rubbing his nose. His eyes were glazed over from a coke-induced euphoria. Not only was he the son of the city's don, he was a don himself. He felt, therefore he acted, invincible.

"Ay yo, ma, what up? Make it clap one time for a nigguh," Tariq urged as the waitress brought over a bottle of the most expensive champagne.

"I'm not a stripper," she replied with measured sass.

"Come on, shorty," Tariq said, cracking a dimpled smile and pulling out a wad of money. He licked his thumb and counted off five 100 dollar bills. That helped them a lot.

"Five hundred. Just show me them pretty titties and get your eagle on. It wasn't only the five hundred that convinced her. Tariq was Santiago's son in more ways than one. He not only inherited his temper, he also inherited his curly hair and light brown eyes that shimmered like brown liquor when the sun reflected through them. Besides, she knew who he was, and since she still believed in fairy tales . . .

She put the bottle on the table, then without hesitation, pulled up her shirt and dropped down in a sexy squat position, coming up slow, showing Tariq what could be his if he said the word.

"Goddamn, shorty! Hol' up, hol' up, I got two more for you. Do it again?"

His entourage whooped and hollered as Tariq handed her the money.

"What I tell you, duke? They all have a price." He chuckled, talking to his man next to him. Then he picked up the bottle of Moet. "I didn't order this."

"I know. That guy over there sent it over. He said it's on him," the waitress explained, pointing to a table across the room.

Three men sat at the table, and as soon as Tariq laid eyes on them, the smile left his face. The playfulness left his aura, and the cocaine in his veins turned to lava.

"Fuckin' Rosario trash!" he mumbled as he locked eyes with the man in the middle.

Antonio Rosario was the youngest of the three Rosario Brothers, Santiago's deadliest rivals. They were straight Cuban killers, and they saw Santiago's operation as their only obstacle to dominating the city. He had sent the bottle, not as a sign of respect, but a sign of disrespect. One, Tariq wasn't about to let go.

The table got quiet as Tariq's crew saw what was happening.

"What you wanna do, God?" Nazir asked, glaring at the three men, too.

It was a good thing no one was armed. The strip club was owned by a friend of Santiago, and Santiago had promised him his people would never violate his establishment. Only tonight Tariq was about to make him a liar.

"Chill. I'ma handle this," Tariq replied.

He got up, grabbing the bottle at the same time and started across the room. Antonio watched with an amused expression as Tariq approached the table. He and Tariq were the same age, eighteen and arrogant, so the rivalry between them was fueled by nothing more than a question: which of the two young men was truly the city's young don?

"I like the other waitress better. She was cuter," Antonio quipped snidely, making his two goons chuckle.

"Nigguh, I sell crack. I don't smoke it. I give cheap ass shit like this to bitches like you," Tariq shot back.

Antonio's two goons tensed.

"Yo, Riq, no disrespect. It was just my way of sayin' hi. The city been good to me." Antonio smirked.

"Man, fuck you!" Tariq grumbled, then turned as if he was about to walk away.

"Fuck wit—" was all Antonio said before Tariq switched his grip on the bottle and swung it in an arc across the table.

He moved so fast, neither goon had time to react. The bottle caught Antonio on the bridge of his nose, breaking it instantly. The goon sitting on his left and closest to Tariq hit Tariq with a straight right jab that staggered him, but that was all he got in before Tariq's crew swarmed the three of them, many of them wielding bottles as well. The three men didn't stand a chance. They were being stomped and beaten bloody.

Tariq straddled a dazed Antonio, sitting on his chest and grabbing a handful of his shirt.

"You . . . bitch . . . ass . . . motherfuckin' faggot!" Tariq cursed, emphasizing every word with a blood-drawing blow.

Tariq began to reach in his pants, but was stopped as the club's security team came in like S.W.A.T. There may have been only four of them, but they were all cock diesel and outweighed all eight of Tariq and his crew. They snatched them up before they knew what hit them.

"Get the fuck outta here now, Tariq!" the head bouncer bassed.

Back in his right state of mind, Tariq knew he has fucked up. He wasn't scared of the bouncer, or the approaching police sirens. He feared Santiago.

When he got home, Santiago was waiting for him in the large, plush living room of the family estate. He sat in the high back leather chair with his legs crossed and a drink in hand, balanced on his knee.

Tariq walked in and shut the door quietly behind him, then looked at Santiago. "I know I fucked up, I know. But that fuckin' Rosario nigguh, Antonio sent a fuckin' bottle—"

Santiago cut him off by simply holding up his hand. He sipped his drink then said, "What I tell you, eh? What I tell you about buts?"

Tariq dropped his head. "Everything after but is bullshit. Never justify your mistakes."

"Exactly. Now . . . tell me what happened," Santiago replied.

Tariq shrugged. "He sent me a bottle of Moet, and I broke his nose with it."

"And for that you were going to shoot him?" Santiago questioned.

"Shoot him?" Tariq echoed with a scowl. "I didn't have a gun."

"So why were you reaching in your pants? Mike said you were reaching."

"I was gonna piss in the nigguh's face."

Santiago shook his head and downed his drink. "I don't need this shit," he mumbled as he put the glass down and struggled to his feet.

Tariq noticed Santiago's swaying. *Is Pop drunk?* He knew something was wrong because Santiago never got drunk.

"Pop, you're drunk?" Tariq remarked, astonished.

"Yeah, but you're the one acting like it," Santiago slurred. "What the fuck you think, huh? You think this is a movie, huh? Some fuckin' rap video and you playin' gangsta. Do you?"

"No, I'm—"

"Every time with you, every time you think the gun is the answer. You put that shit up your nose, and you think you fuckin' Scarface," Santiago spat, shaking his head.

His thoughts were reeling over his broken family. His son was a line of coke away from being an addict; his wife fucking around in the street like a common whore, and his cousin betraying him. All he could do was grab his head.

"Pop, are you okay?" Tariq questioned, stepping toward him.

Santiago's glare froze him in his tracks. "Get the fuck outta my face, Tariq! . . . Now!" he growled.

Tariq turned and left the room.

Santiago staggered from the room in the other direction. They say things come in threes, so after hearing about his wife and son, he was waiting on the last straw.

As he rounded the corner, he saw the light under his daughter Eva's door still on. He stopped and knocked.

"Come in," she sang.

Santiago smiled as he entered. "What do you mean, come in? Aren't you supposed to ask who is it first? What if I was Jason or somebody?"

Eve looked up from her laptop and giggled. "Daddy, I'm seventeen. I don't believe in boogey men anymore. Besides, who else could it be but family?" She had such a trusting heart, not knowing it was family that you most often had to beware of. He stood in the door, beaming at his little angel. Eva was the perfect blend of her mother and him. She had light bronze skin like him, but her mother's soft, feminine features. Eva looked like a young Selma Hayek. She sat on her bed, Indian style, with her laptop on her lap and her glasses perched on the end of her nose. She pushed the glasses up with her index finger and Santiago chuckled.

"You're such a blerd," he remarked.

"A what?"

"A blerd, a black nerd." He chuckled drunkenly, but with good nature.

Eve rolled her eyes playfully. "Daddy, that's not a word."

"It is now. I just made it up," he replied and sat beside her on the edge of the bed.

"You can't make words up."

"Sure you can. How do you think words exist in the first place?"

Eve started to agree, but then the alcohol stench hit her and she wrinkled up her nose. "Daddy, have you been drinking?"

He shrugged, put his arm around her neck, and then kissed the top of her head. "I just have a lot on my mind, baby girl."

She cuddled up next to him. "Then you should pray. God will take care of it."

"I'm scared to go to the church. I'd probably burst into flames." He laughed.

Eva shook her head.

When his laughter subsided, he tilted her head to look at him. "You're the only one I trust," he said solemnly.

"Trust for what?" she asked.

Before he could answer, Mel appeared in the doorway. Santiago looked up at her and caught a chill as his hate and his love battled within him. As mad as he was at her, his heart couldn't help but admire her. She was a goddess. Black, bold, and beautiful. She looked like Gabrielle U but a tad darker. So dark, she shined naturally. Mel was clad in an Atlanta Falcons jersey. Her long, bare, thick chocolate legs looked delicious. She folded her arms and looked at Eva. "You're supposed to be in bed."

"I couldn't sleep. I wanted to work on my computer program," Eva whined.

Mel sucked her teeth and came in. She took the laptop and abruptly shut it off.

"Ma! I didn't save that!" Eva gasped.

"You're so smart, you can do it again," Mel spat back sarcastically and put the laptop on the table.

Eva sucked her teeth.

"Do it again and you won't have nothin' to suck," Mel snapped.

Eva held her tongue and got in bed.

Santiago kissed her on the forehead. "Your mother's right. It's late. We'll talk manana."

"Okay, Daddy. Tomorrow."

Mel and Santiago walked toward her door. "So you're drinkin now?" she asked.

"Does it matter?" he shot back.

Eva hopped out of bed and approached them from behind. "Daddy. Ma. Please don't fight. Please don't," Eva asked with pleading, shimmery eyes.

Santiago and Mel both turned to look at Eva. "We're just talking, my little blerd. Guess we gotta bring the tone down, un poco." Her father's gesture with his index finger and thumb plus his doting smile, put Eva at ease. The blank stare she received from her mother, however, sent her rushing back toward her bed.

The couple made their exit. Santiago gently shut Eva's door before glaring down at Mel. Seeing the look on his face, she knew not to push it. When they got to the bedroom, she helped him out of his shoes. Mel reached for his pants, and he grabbed her wrists.

"What's wrong, baby? You okay?" she asked sweetly.

"Everything I do is for this family. You know that, right?" Santiago sat upright on the bed while Mel stood over him.

"I know," she replied.

Slowly, he let her hand go. She reached out and caressed his cheek. "Tell me what's wrong, baby?"

Santiago looked into her eyes and replied, "Why would something be wrong? Is it?" His heart ached, but his ego wouldn't allow him to admit it, even to himself.

Mel's eyes registered something unsettling just beyond the surface, but she quickly covered it with a compassionate gaze that Santiago's drunken mind failed to catch on to.

"Everything's okay, baby," Mel cooed, kissing his eyelids, then his nose. Finally, she settled on his lips, sucking his bottom one, and then slipping her tongue in his mouth.

Her tongue tasted extra sweet to Santiago, as if the poison that tipped it were made of honey. Her soft hands roamed his body, then slid into his boxers and gripped his fat dick. She gave it a squeeze, teasing it into a semi-erection, then took it out and kissed it.

Santiago watched her kissing his dick, but his mind was blinded by the thought of her kissing and caressing Alex's dick in the same way. He watched her wrap her full sexy lips around the head, but again, in his mind it was Alex. He couldn't shake it. The semi-erection deflated in her hands.

Mel looked up at him and stood to her feet quietly. She knew why he couldn't get hard, and the thought that was clouding his mind. But deep down part of her felt he deserved it. After all the years of having to deal with the other women, and the lonely nights when she knew he was lying in the next bitch's bed. Now she had found a man who loved her, and indirectly, Santiago now knew how it felt too. He may have been her heart, but her lover was a guilty pleasure.

"You know I love you, right?" Santiago said, caressing her cheek with his fingertips.

"I know," she replied, biting her bottom lip seductively.

He pulled her up to lay her head on his chest and hold her tight. His ego wouldn't allow him to name the elephant in the room, and his love wouldn't allow him to let her go.

Santiago was caught up.

Chapter 3

Trouble Times Two

I'm tellin' you, unc, the bitch a strange freak! Look at that ass!" Tariq exclaimed, showing Alex the fifteen second video of a chick bent over in the mirror fingering herself with four fingers and looking over her shoulder making fuck faces.

Alex took the phone and played the video again.

"Damn, she thick as fuck. She look like that porn star Cherokee," he remarked.

Tariq popped a French fry in his mouth.

"And she only sixteen, yo. I turned that little bitch out!"

Alex scowled and quickly handed Tariq his phone back. "Goddamn, nephew! You tryin' to get me locked up? She ain't even legal," Alex gruffed.

Tariq shrugged and tucked his phone in his pocket. "Man, fuck that. That bitch a porn star waitin' to happen."

Alex looked around the McDonald's as he sipped his milkshake. They were sitting in the back of the restaurant. It was midday, but this particular McDonalds in the hood didn't do a brisk lunch crowd.

"Oh yo! What ever happened to that white bitch you said you were gonna turn me on to?" Tariq questioned.

"I ain't seen that bitch in a minute. I've been fuckin' with this . . . married broad," Alex admitted with a sly grin Tariq didn't quite catch.

"Yeah, married pussy the best. Fuck her and send her home." Tariq laughed.

"Naw yo." Alex sipped his milkshake. "I got plans for this one."

Tariq checked his watch. "Yo, where these nigguhs at? I thought you told 'em two o'clock."

"I did. Hold up, I'm a hit 'em again," Alex replied, pulling out his phone and standing up.

"Where you goin'?"

"Outside. I can never get a fuckin' signal here," Alex answered, moving his phone around, looking for bars.

Alex walked outside while Tariq finished off his burger. He checked his own phone and he didn't have a decent signal either. "Damn!" he grumbled.

When he looked up from his phone, three suspect-looking dudes entered McDonald's. They spotted him way in the back and headed in his direction. Tariq took his eyes off them long enough to look at Alex right outside the door. He appeared to be talking to someone. Instantly, Tariq's street sense kicked in. As he once again focused to his left, the three guys pulled out fully automatic pistols. Tariq dove under the table just as the first barrage of bullets ripped through the wood and vinyl of the booth.

Brrrr! Brrrrrrrr!

Gunfire erupted as mothers grabbed kids and ran off screaming. Alex heard the gunfire and tried to come back in, but one of the gun men aimed at the door, making Alex dive behind a car. Tariq, without looking up, raised his gun and returned fire.

Boc! Boc! Boc!

The gunmen were in the middle of the aisle, so the shots scattered them to take cover in booths. Tariq leaned down and peeked under the booth, seeing a pair of legs within close distance. He let off a bombardment of shots, shattering the exposed ankles.

"Aaaaaaarrrrggh! Fuck!" the hit man cried out.

That was all Tariq needed. He popped up quickly and blasted twice. The dude he had hit in the ankle had sat up in pain, exposing himself. The next shot put him out of his misery, blowing off the top of his head like a popped zit.

Meanwhile, Alex had come around the front of the restaurant and pinned the remaining two gunmen in. One gun man noticed him and took aim, but to do so he opened himself up to Tariq, who didn't waste the opportunity.

Boc! Boc!

One shot caught him in the neck, spinning him off balance. Alex ran up and finished him with a straight shot to the dome that blew his face through the back of his head.

The third and final gun man sat back, pistol empty. When Tariq ran up on him, he threw up both hands.

"Don't shoot, yo, don't shoot! Rosario sent me. It's just the game!" he cried.

"Yeah, well, I'm sending you back," Tariq spat, then gave him three point blank, ensuring his funeral would be a closed casket.

"Let's go!" Alex barked.

They flew out the rear door and headed for Tariq's black on black Maserati.

"No!" Alex blurted. The sound of sirens wailed as if they were right on top of them. "Run!"

Tariq agreed with Alex's advice, and they both dashed off, dipping into the alley and behind the dumpster seconds before a swarm of police pulled into the parking lot.

The two of them jumped the fence along the back of McDonald's and came out on the next street.

"The bus stop!" Tariq said, nodding at the next corner.

Checking over their shoulder, they headed for the bus stop. It took a couple of minutes, but to them it felt like hours. They both knew if the police had seen them make their escape, they'd be swarmed any second.

Finally, the bus came and they hurried inside. As the bus lurched off, both of them ran their pockets for change but found none. The bus driver looked at them. Alex handed him a fifty.

"Keep the change." Alex winked.

"Damn sho' will," the bus driver replied, stuffing the bill in his pocket. Alex and Tariq went to the back of the bus and sat down.

"What the fuck just happened?" Alex remarked, keeping his voice low.

"Rosario," Tariq growled, punching his fist, temperature on blaze.

"I know that, but that's how they bringin' it now?"

"Naw yo. I stomped Antonio bitch ass out in the club last night. This him tryin' to get his get back. I'm a kill that muhfucka!" Tariq bassed.

"Yo, yo chill, chill," Alex reminded him, then added, "you told Santiago!"

"Yeah."

"What he say?"

"Nothin'."

"Nothin'?"

Tariq looked at him. "Fuckin' nothing. He was drunk."

Alex's eyes got wide. "Santiago drunk?"

Tariq nodded.

Alex shook his head. "Yo, your father ain't just my cousin. I love him like a brother, but goddamn . . ." He shook his head again. "He startin' to slip."

Tariq looked at Alex. Besides his father, Alex and Basim were the only men he looked up to, so when they spoke, he listened.

"What you mean?"

Alex looked around, then replied, "Come on, let's get off."

At the next stop they got off the bus. As the roar of the bus engine lessened, Alex said, "Them Rosario muhfuckas been pushin' up on us hard. Even down in the South, yo. That's why I've been gettin' our guns right down there. It's gonna be a war."

"You goddamn right it is!" Tariq barked. "These muhfuckas just tried to kill me!"

"Yeah, but Santiago been on some chill shit lately. All he talk about is going legit. He been lettin' them Rosario nigguhs get too bold," Alex remarked, eyeing Tariq's reaction.

Tariq was soaking it up like a sponge. "No doubt, but yo, I know he gonna wanna move now. They just fucked up!"

"Yeah, but it's gonna have to come from you, Riq. You have to holla at Santiago. He'll listen to you. Legit is cool, but we ain't gotta fuckin' let that trash take over, feel me, nephew?"

Tariq gave him a pound and a gangsta hug. "I got you, unc. I'm a holla at him asap."

Alex nodded. "Tambien. Handle yo' biz. And be careful when you go back for your car."

"Don't worry, I'ma send a bitch to get it," Tariq assured him.

"Cool. I'm out."

They hugged once more, then went their separate ways. As Alex walked, he felt a little guilty getting in Tariq's head to go at Santiago, but he knew for his plan to work, he had to have Santiago's ear.

His phone rang. He pulled out the phone and looked at the number. Alex frowned slightly because he didn't recognize the number, but he answered anyway. "Yo."

"Alex? This is Mel."

"Mel? What's good?"

"I need to see you right away . . . it's important"

"I'm on my way."

"No, not here. I'll call you . . . okay?"

She hung up.

"What the fuck was that all about?" Alex asked, scratching his head. The McDonald's shooting had been enough action for one day. He sensed trouble the minute Mel stated her name."

Chapter 4

Wrapped Around Her Finger

(Mel's Story)

Twenty years ago...

Little girl, can you hear me? Everything's okay now. I'm a cop, okay? Can you hear me? Do you know what happened? Who did this?"

The voice of the officer sounded so far away to Mel, as if it were coming from another world. It had to be another world because hers had been shattered. The twelve-year-old girl had just become an orphan. She sat shivering, even though it was a hot summer Brooklyn night. Shivering and covered in blood. Her flimsy cotton nightgown stuck to her because of the blood, sweat, and tears. The blood belonged to her parents', but the sweat and tears were hers.

They had only been in America for a few months, having been forced to leave Jamaica. Her father, Thomas was a local organizer in the JLP-controlled Tivoli Garden

Projects. The JLP, or Jamaican Labor Party, was one of the main two political parties on the island. In Jamaica, everything is connected to politics, even life or death. Already a very violent country, the murder rate soared every election night, so when the People National Party won the election, Mel's father knew he was in danger. He and his family fled the island.

But escape wouldn't be that easy . . .

Mel's father, Thomas, was an enforcer in the JLP, one who knew too many secrets, one who couldn't be allowed to live. They tracked him to Bed-Stuy to bring Jamaican-styled justice to America.

"Not in front of my family!" Thomas pleaded when they bum-rushed the small apartment.

"Stop yer blood clot cryin'!" one of the three masked men hissed as he brought his machete up and over his head.

Mel would never forget the way the blade glistened in the moonlight, just before the dread-headed monster hacked into the flesh of her father' throat. The blade was so sharp, that one swing nearly decapitated him. Thomas's body slumped to the floor as Mel's mother grabbed her and covered her body with her own.

"I love you, Melanie," her mother said, looking into her eyes right before the blade hacked away half her face.

Mel was too stunned to scream. The men hacked away viciously over and over, severing limbs and slicing flesh from bone. This was meant to be more than a murder, it was a message.

When they finished, the one room apartment was splattered with blood. The men, winded by their wicked work, looked down at the girl curled up in a puddle of her mother's blood.

"Wha gwan do wi de pickaninny?" one of the men asked.

The tallest killer looked down at her, his head tilted slightly. He ran the tip of his bloody machete down her tender curves. Even at twelve, her blossom to come was very evident.

He put the blade under her cheek and turned her face to look at him. He looked into her eyes and couldn't bring himself to kill such beauty.

"Jah bless, our work is done 'eh," he commanded, then turned for the door.

In her mind, she could still feel the cold steel of the machete, or what her father used to call the cutlass. For a few days it was all she could feel. She didn't feel the ambulance worker pick her up, nor the movement of the ambulance as they transferred her to the hospital. It was three days before the world began to seep into her stupor.

One of the first things she heard was her social worker talking on her phone.

"Yes, I think that would be best. Miss Brooks runs an upstanding foster home, one where I think Mel will be well received with good Christian love."

"Jah bless . . ." the social worker said, ending the call.

Mel, however, heard the voice of her father's killer in her head.

Miss Brooks looked like Florida Evans from the TV show *Good Times*. Short and dumpy, with a graying tight afro and a warm, heartfelt smile punctuated with a gold tooth. As soon as she laid eyes on Mel, she wrapped her in a big motherly hug.

"Lord ha' mercy child, how are you? What's your name?" Miss Brooks asked, cradling Mel's cheeks in her big, soft hands.

Mel just looked up at her shyly.

"Her name is Melanie Verley. Here's her file. She's been through a very traumatic experience," her social worker explained.

Miss Brooks took the file, but said, "All I need to know is right here in these big brown eyes. Don't worry, baby. The Lord will fix this," she concluded, kissing Mel on the forehead.

The first few days, Mel kept to herself. Miss Brooks had four other girls. Amy, a brown-haired, scrawny white girl who was fifteen, Lisa, a fourteen-year-old black girl and two Spanish girls, Maria and Louisa, both fourteen. They were all nice to her, making her feel at home just like Big Mama, as they affectionately called her.

A month later on the night Mel drank the milk . . .

"You want some warm milk, baby?" Miss Brooks had asked Mel, because she was having nightmares.

"Yes, ma'am," Mel answered.

"What I tell you 'bout that ma'am stuff?" Miss Brooks scolded her gently.

"Yes . . . Big Mama."

Miss Brooks smiled big and warm. "That's better." She set the cup in front of Mel and patted her cheek. "Drink up, sweetie."

Mel did.

Oxytocin is a chemical released by the human body. It is usually associated with sexual bonding, affection . . . orgasms. Many try to use it as a date rape drug, but it's not. Oxytocin cannot be used to create sexual bonds. It can only be used to enhance bonds already forming.

As Mel drank her milk, Miss Brooks stroked her long, silky ponytails. "I know you've been through a lot, child, but believe me, the Lord is gonna make it right," Miss Brooks cooed.

"Yes, Big Mama," Mel replied, feeling warm and toasty. She liked how Miss Brooks' hand felt in her hair, then how it felt on her back. It was sooooo comforting.

She finished the oxytocin-laced milk. Miss Brooks took the cup. "Ready for bed?"

Mel nodded.

Miss Brooks beamed. "Okay. You can sleep with me. The Lord keeps away all those bad nightmares."

When they got into Miss Brook's queen-sized bed, she wrapped Mel up in a tight embrace and laid her head on her ample bosom. Miss Brooks stroked her back. "Such a beautiful girl . . . So lovely . . . So tender . . . yesss, the Lord is gonna take a good care of you."

As she spoke, her caress went from comforting to sensual, teasing the back of Mel's neck down to her hips and around to her small but pert breasts.

Mel had never been touched sexually before, but the oxytocin and Miss Brook's subtle approach made it feel like a natural progression.

"That feel good, baby?"

"Ye–yes, Big Mama," Mel cooed, her body tingling in ways that both scared and aroused her at the same time.

Miss Brooks had expert hands. She knew how to turn a young girl out because she herself had been turned out as a young girl. She knew just where to kiss, just where to lick, to make a young girl's teeth chatter and get her pussy wet for the first time.

When Mel felt Miss Brook's tongue in her pussy, she arched her back and pushed her head deep into the pillow. Many nights she had heard the sounds of moans and pleasure-filled screams coming from Miss Brook's room, but she never knew what it was. Now she did, because she was the one moaning.

"Lawd chile, your pussy tastes sweeter than mangoes," Miss Brooks remarked as she feasted on Mel's clit.

"Ohhh, Big Mama," Mel groaned, having her first orgasm all over Miss Brook's mouth.

Miss Brooks reached under the bed and pulled out a long black dildo. Mel's body tensed up when she saw it. Miss Brooks smiled.

"Don't worry, baby, this won't hurt. This . . . is the Lord and I told you, the Lord is gonna take real good care of you."

She rubbed the rubber head against Mel's clit, curling Mel's toes. She spread Mel's legs and slid the dildo inside of her. Mel's breath caught in her throat. The dildo slid up easily inside her wet, virgin pussy. Mel cried out in ecstasy, her head thrashing from side to side.

"Take it out! Take it out! It's too—" Mel begged, until the thin membrane within her popped and sent her over the edge from a girl to a woman.

Now, each long stroke created a rhythm that Mel's body couldn't help but dance to.

"You like that, don't you?"

"Mmm . . . mmmm," Mel moaned, meeting each thrust with one of her own.

"Yeah, baby, you a good one. You gonna make Big Mama a lot of money, ain't you?" Miss Brooks sang.

"Yesssssss," Mel replied, as her body convulsed and release her young nectar.

It would be the first of many, but to Mel's immature mind, one time was too much and a million times is never enough.

After that night, Mel would never see the world the same again. She looked at her house mates different as well. They became her rivals for Miss Brooks' affection, especially Maria. She was by far the most beautiful. Mel was a knockout too, but she would never get over Maria's soft caramel complexion and long. wavy hair.

She despised Maria.

"I'll get it, Big Mama," Mel offered one day as they traversed the aisles of a local grocery store.

She and Maria had gone with her to help her shop. Mel skipped off to get Miss Brooks the pork chops she requested, but while she was in the next section, she saw some fish. Mel loved fish. She grabbed the pack and skipped back to the cart.

"Big Mama, can we get this, too? I love fish," Mel pleaded.

Miss Brooks smiled indulgently, but replied, "I'm sorry, baby, but Maria is allergic to seafood."

"Well, she don't have to eat it," Mel pouted.

"No, baby, put it back. I'll get you something else."

Maria's smile said, 'I'm more important' to Mel's immature, jealous mind. Miss Brooks knew the rivalry between Mel and Maria, so she used it to her advantage. Especially since it was time to put Mel to work.

"Lord ha' mercy, I just don't know what I'm gonna do," Miss Brooks said two days later, while reclining on her bed reading the mail. Mel sat at the other end watching TV.

"What's wrong, Big Mama?" Mel asked, looking over her shoulder. Miss Brooks shook her head.

"It's them people. They cut in the money I get to keep all you girls. With what I'ma be gettin', I'm not gonna be able to keep everybody . . . and since you are the last . . ."

Before she had finished her statement, Mel leapt from her end of the bed to Miss Brook's lap, tears already streaming down her face.

"Please, Big Mama, don't send me away! Please, where I'm gonna go? I love you!" She wrapped her scrawny little arms around Miss Brook's neck.

Miss Brooks smiled to herself. She had used the tactic on countless girls, and it hadn't failed yet. From loving mother to lesbian lover, she was ready to become the cold-blooded pimp she truly was.

"I just don't see how—"

"I–I'll work. I'll get a job!" Mel offered.

Miss Brooks chuckled. "Baby, you're too young to work. But maybe . . . No, no, it's too much," Miss Brooks mused, toying with Mel's mind.

"No, no! I'll do it, I'll do it! I'll do anything, just don't send me away," Mel sobbed.

"It's a job for a big girl. No, maybe I'll get Maria . . ."

Mel's eyes glazed over with sheer hate.

"No!" she seethed, "I said I'll do it!"

Hook, line, and sinker, Miss Brooks thought with smile full of mischief. She then kissed Mel on the forehead.

"I'll make the call."

*****

"Don't be scared, Melanie. I'm not going to hurt you. I like you."

Mel didn't say anything. She stared at the small, white, scrawny and shriveled man. His hairline was receding, and he looked like a school teacher. He was a school teacher, and he fantasized about the little girls in his fifth grade class, so Mel was perfect. She was truly a dream come true.

They occupied a room in the rundown Bristol Hotel in Queens. Large roaches roamed the stained walls in room 515 without fear. They made Mel's skin crawl, but the feeling of his clammy hands touching her was worse.

"Did you do your homework?" he asked with a quiver in his voice.

"What!" she answered, aggravation in hers.

"Your homework . . . play along," he told her.

She remembered why she was there. *Big Mama.*

"What do you want me to say?"

"No."

"No," she repeated.

He leered. "Then you must be punished. Take off your clothes."

She did as she was told. When she was totally naked, he shivered with delight. "My God, you are beautiful. Yes, you must be punished badly." He took her by the arm and laid her across his lap, then slapped her hard on the ass.

"Owwwww!" she cried out in pain.

His dick boned instantly. He spanked her again and she cried out louder. After several slaps, he came in his pants.

"Lie on the bed and bend over," he ordered her, and she did.

He pulled out a Polaroid camera and took picture after picture. When he finished, he handed her two hundred dollars.

"Get dressed."

Just like that, her life as a prostitute began. For the next four years, she learned all she needed to know about the nature of a man. She learned to control a man's mind through his genitals, she learned her beauty was her most potent weapon, and she learned money was her only love.

Quickly she became Miss Brook's top earner. Mel saw girls come and go. The only one who remained was Maria. No matter what, she couldn't take her place with Miss Brooks. So instead, she stopped trying and decided to remove her once and for all. It would all be over the following day.

"Don't worry, Tricia, I'll cook that spaghetti for you," Mel offered with a surprising smile around dinnertime.

Tricia was the new girl, a fifteen-year-old Greek, who was eager to please. "No, that's okay. I've got it."

"No really . . . let me. Don't tell Big Mama I told you, but she doesn't really like your cooking. She just doesn't want to hurt your feelings," Mel lied.

Tricia was crushed. She liked Miss Brooks. She didn't want to disappoint her.

"I'll tell you what. I'll fix it and you can say you cooked it. Deal?" Mel offered.

"Deal." Tricia giggled, then left the kitchen.

As soon as she was gone, Mel pulled out the plastic bag from her pocket, ground up salt fish and quickly stirred it up and dumped it in the pot of spaghetti.

That night, when Maria sat down to eat, she got the surprise of her life. "Tricia, this spaghetti is deli—" she started to say, until she felt a strange tickle in her throat. Suddenly she felt light-headed, and she had the overwhelming urge to cough. But when she did, nothing came out. Her airway began to constrict as her neck began to swell.

"Oh my God! Maria, are you okay?" Tricia cried when she saw her face turning blue.

Mel jumped up. "She's choking!" she exclaimed, knowing that Maria wasn't. She grabbed her as if to give her the Heimlich maneuver, but in her mind, really trying to buy time to let the fish do its work.

"She ain't chokin'! It's an allergic reaction," Miss Brooks barked as she rushed into the kitchen.

She heard Tricia cry out Maria's name and came running. Quickly she called 911, and after forcing milk down Maria's throat, got her stabilized enough to survive until EMS arrived. Miss Brooks hadn't been fooled. She knew exactly what had happened.

"Mel . . . you have to go," Miss Brooks told her three days later when she called her into her room.

"Big Mama, why?" Mel cried.

Miss Brooks sat stone-faced and unmoved by her tears. "Bitch, you know damn well why," she hissed. "I run a respectable establishment, and I damn sure don't need no goddamn bodies droppin' 'round here."

"No, Big Mama, please. I won't do it again!" Mel sobbed, throwing herself around Miss Brook's ample waist.

Miss Brooks hugged her back, but replied, "Girl, I love you. Lawd knows I do. But you dangerous. You can't be trusted. Ain't nothin' you won't do to get what you want."

Mel looked at her, the tears still wet but her gaze was cold. "Ain't that what you taught me?"

"No baby, it was already there." Miss Brooks shook her head. "I just brought it out. Don't worry, you'll be okay. You just can't be here no mo'. Now pack your shit. I want you gone by the morning." With that, Miss Brooks turned and walked away.

For four years of service, Miss Brooks gave her five hundred dollars and a suitcase full of clothes. From that experience, Mel learned to always control the money.

In the next two months, Mel was raped several times as she tried to sell her body, but she only knew how to be a whore, not a pimp. She sat in the Chinese restaurant one night waiting for her order. Thoughts of suicide clouded her mind. Inside, she was torn apart. Missing Big Mama, hating Big Mama, needing Big Mama's guidance. But on the outside, she was a bad bitch waiting to happen.

That's what Santiago saw.

Tasha Macklin

From the moment he laid eyes on her, he knew he had to make her his. The moment she laid eyes on him, she knew she'd have him wrapped around her finger.

Chapter 4

Think Before You Move

He had her pinned against the wall, her legs wrapped around his waist, and his dick deep inside her tight, wet pussy. Angel's dick felt so good inside of Eva, she wanted him to keep fucking her forever. Especially after the blunt of exotic they had just smoked.

Angel spread her soft, juicy ass cheeks and penetrated her puckered hole with the tip of his middle finger, something he knew drove Eva crazy.

"Oh fuck! You kn-know that's my sssspot." She melted, sucking on his bottom lip while she bounced on his dick.

"Your pussy feels so good," he grunted.

"Tell me again," she gasped.

"Your pussy feels so good."

She bounced harder, fighting to hold in her squeal so no one would hear her. "Oh my God, Angel, I'm about to cum!"

"Cum for me, baby," he urged.

"Oh, I am! I am. I—" Her breath caught in her throat as she released hard, long and creamy.

Her body trembled in the aftermath, as Angel released his shot, filling the condom. His knees sagged and Eva put her feet down.

"Let me get down before you drop me." She giggled.

"Shit!" Angel exclaimed, beads of sweat popping off his forehead. "If your pops could see your goody two-shoes ass now, huh?" he joked.

"Shut up," she said, punching him playfully. "It'll be worse for you. He'd kill you, but I'm daddy's little girl." She winked.

Eva smoothed down her skirt. Then she checked her watch. "Oh shit! Let me go. I know Tariq will be here any minute." She pecked Angel on his lips, but he pulled her to him.

"You gonna call me?" he questioned.

"No." She pecked him again. "But I bet you call me."

Angel smirked. "Oh word! It's like that?"

"Stop playin', with your insecure ass. You know I'ma call you, boy," she assured him. As she turned away, he slapped her on the ass.

"You better."

She licked her tongue out, then walked to the bathroom door. She peeked out, and seeing the coast was clear, blew Angel a kiss over her shoulder then quickly exited.

"There that bitch go!"

Eva turned in the direction of the shout and saw four girls approaching. She knew them all, especially the tallest girl in the middle, Kim. She was on the cheerleader squad and hated Eva's guts. It wasn't that she felt Eva looked better, because on paper, they looked like twins. Both were mixed, both had Egyptian bronze skin and long hair and both had banging bodies. But Eva had that certain something that, deep down, Kim knew she lacked.

She stepped up to Eva just as Angel emerged from the bathroom.

"I know y'all ain't just finish fuckin'! I just know y'all ain't just finish fuckin!" Kim ranted, bouncing on the balls of her feet like she was ready to pounce.

"Ay yo, Kim—" Angel started to say, but she cut him off.

"And you, just shut up because I've just about had it with you," she huffed.

Angel got silent.

"Mmm hmm!"

"You tell him, Kim!"

"Handle your biz, girl!" Her choir sang in the background.

Emboldened by the crowd, she turned back to Eva and shoved her. "Did you just fuck my man, bitch?"

If he was your man, he wasn't just now, went the voice in Eva's head, but as always she ignored it and replied, "Look Kim, I don't want any problems."

Kim scoffed. "You should've thought of that before you opened your goddamn legs!" Kim barked, punctuating her statement with a sneaky right jab.

The punch hardly fazed Eva because Tariq had taught her how to roll with the punch. He had taught her many boxing techniques, but Eva never used them because she hated violence. Whenever someone would pick on her, her insides would rage like there was a beast trapped inside, but she wouldn't let it out. Even when Kim knocked her to the ground and the voice in her head kept screaming, 'I'ma kill this bitch!' Eva just balled up and took the beating with nary a whimper. Kim kicked her in the stomach and knocked the wind out of her.

"Next time, bitch, I'ma really fuck you up! Stay away from Angel!" Kim ordered, standing over Eva triumphantly.

"Come on, girl. Let's go. She don't want it," one of the girls said.

"Come on, Angel," Kim told him. "Angel!" she repeated more firmly.

"I–I'm sorry," he mumbled to Eva then headed off behind Kim.

Eva lay on the floor, trying to catch her breath. *One day I'll get her*, she seethed as she watched the crowd walk away. "It's over," she mumbled.

After a brief struggle to stand, Eva headed out the gym door deciding she wouldn't even tell her best friend Asia about this fight with Kim.

Outside, Tariq and several bodyguards were waiting by a stretch black Benz limousine. Tariq was pacing back and forth in front of the limo, checking and double checking his watch. The bodyguards were spread out, keeping their eyes peeled. When Tariq finally spotted her, he rushed over. A Lincoln Navigator was parked right behind it.

"What took you so long? I thought practice was over at four?" he questioned, then turned to one of the bodyguards and said, "Tell Mat we got her."

The bodyguard got on his cell and relayed the message while Tariq walked Eva to the car.

"I–I lost track of time," Eva stuttered.

"And why is your face so red and what's this scratch? Eva, I know those girls ain't been pickin' on you," Tariq growled, ready to smack fire out of the high school girls.

"No, it happened in practice," she lied as she got in the limo. Tariq got in behind her and shut the door. Some of the bodyguards got in front and some got in the black Lincoln Navigator, bringing up the rear.

"Stop playin' with me, Eva," Tariq warned.

"It's nothing, okay? Just let it go. And why all the bodyguards? What's going on?"

"Shit got heated earlier. Muhfuckas tried to kill me, but they missed," Tariq replied arrogantly.

"Oh my God, Tariq! Why?" she gasped.

"Long story."

Eva sighed hard and shook her head. "I need a blunt."

Tariq pulled one out and lit it. He took a pull, then passed it to her. Eva inhaled deeply and her body visibly relaxed.

"Now, are you gonna tell me what happened?" Tariq probed. "And don't say practice, unless you're practicin' to be a fuckin' welcome mat," he spat, pointing to the shoe print on Eva's shirt.

"Tariq, please, let it go. It's dead," she explained.

Tariq flexed his jaw muscles trying to calm himself. "Baby girl, when are you gonna learn? You have to protect yourself!"

"I know, Tariq, I know . . . I just . . . hate violence. That's all it is with our family, and I'm sick of it."

"It's a violent world, Eva. These muhfuckas don't understand anything else."

They rode the rest of the way in silence, each lost in their own world, passing the blunt back and forth. Once they got home, a guy of average height stood near a BMW with his arms crossed.

"Who's that, Tariq?" Eva asked, squinting to get a better view.

Tariq lowered the window and took a closer look. "Oh shit! That's my man, Nazir. Stay here until I'm done." Two bodyguards exited the Benz limo first.

"Okay. Your friend's kinda cute," Eva mumbled as Tariq left the vehicle next.

"What did you say, Eva?" Tariq asked, unsure if he'd heard her correctly.

"Nothing. I didn't say anything." She peeped her head through the window and tried unsuccessfully to make eye contact with the guy. Eva didn't want him to see her entire face anyway. Not after the beat down from Kim.

Her brother met with the guy and shook his hand. They exchanged a few words, and the guy hopped in his car and rushed off. The Lincoln Navigator pulled off behind him, and the other two bodyguards returned to the Benz limo.

"C'mon, Eva," Tariq said, walking toward their home. "Let's go inside."

Eva raised the window back up and got out of the vehicle and followed Tariq. They both saw their mother entering the kitchen.

"Oh shit! Mommy's home," Eva said, going in her bag for her sunglasses and breath mints.

Tariq laughed. "Ain't no need in tryin' to cover it up now."

As soon as Mel saw her, she looked right past the fact she was high and zeroed in on her shirt and face. "What happened, Eva?"

"Nothing, Mommy."

"I know nothing, and that ain't it. Some little bitch musta got hold of that ass for thinkin' you so goddamn cute," Mel huffed.

"She ain't cute, she beautiful," a masculine voice said.

Eva turned just as Santiago entered the kitchen. "Hey, Daddy!" Eva beamed, kissing him on the cheek.

"Whateva'!" Mel grumbled.

Eva glanced at her mother out the corner of her eye. She couldn't quite put her finger on it, but it seemed the older she got, the colder Mel acted toward her. *What was her problem?* Eva wondered.

To Mel, Eva looked more and more like Maria.

Mel's phone rang. She looked at the number and walked out of the kitchen with Santiago's eyes glued to her back.

"Daddy . . . Daddy . . . Daddy," Eva said before Santiago could hear her over the tea-kettle whistle in his ears.

"Yeah, baby girl!"

"Are you okay? Why are you looking like that?" she questioned.

Santiago hadn't realized his expression had turned to stone. He lightened it with a smile. "I should ask you the same thing," he replied, taking off her sunglasses and gently caressing the reddened scar on her cheek. "Mama, when are you gonna learn? You can't keep it bottled up, because the longer you wait, the worse it'll be when it explodes." Santiago looked straight into her eyes and spoke directly to the beast within.

Her eyes smiled, but she shook her head. "I'll . . . I'll be okay."

Santiago kissed her forehead. "También."

As he began to walk away, Eva said, "Daddy, what did you mean when you said I'm the only one you can trust?"

He stopped and turned back to her. "I hope we never have to find out," he replied solemnly, then walked out of the kitchen.

*****

"Pop!" Tariq called out to him when Santiago entered the living room.

"What is it, Tariq?"

Tariq approached. "You still haven't given me an answer from earlier."

Santiago sighed and pinched the bridge of his nose. Tariq used the opportunity to continue. "I know you don't want a war. I understand that. But at this point, what else could we do? They declared war in McDonald's today, not us!" Tariq reminded him.

"That wasn't war. That was the result of two young, dumb motherfuckas, you and Antonio, playing a silly ass game that could bring everybody down," Santiago growled. "Now, what I'ma do is speak with the Rosario Brothers and get this thing squashed."

"Speak to them!" Tariq echoed, wide-eyed. "Pop, they tried to kill me! Your son! What's to talk about?"

Even though Tariq was trying his patience, Santiago could see the pain in his eyes, so he took a deep breath. He looked at Tariq with pity in his heart. Tariq wanted to be like his father so bad, but he had only inherited his temper and not his ability to strategize. Deep down Santiago knew Tariq could never run the family, so it was best to make peace . . . for Tariq's own sake.

"Tariq, listen . . . I've told you before, think before you move. You made a foolish move, and now you're dealing with the consequences. You say they declared war? Have you forgotten you were about to piss on the man? Are they supposed to simply accept that?"

"Alex was right," Tariq mumbled.

Hearing Alex's name come out of Tariq's mouth caught Santiago off guard, and all the venom he had for his cousin came out at his son. Santiago almost slapped Tariq, he was so tense.

"I don't care what anyone says! Until a muhfucka proves man enough to take my spot, then I make the goddamn calls! Tu entiende?" The look in his eyes told Tariq not to push it.

"Yeah, yeah, I understand," Tariq grumbled then left the room.

Santiago headed to the bedroom. When he got there, he heard the shower running. Through the open bathroom door he could see her naked silhouette in the frosted shower glass. Even blurred, her figure looked sensual and delicious. The temptation made his head hurt.

He spotted her phone on the nightstand and picked it up. He half expected it to be locked, but when he pressed send, her call list popped up. He scrolled through and saw what he feared most. Several calls to and from Alex. It only confirmed what he knew in his heart . . .

Someone was going to die.

Chapter 5

Murders Don't Matter

As soon as she pulled out of the McDonald's parking lot, she heard the Whoop! Whoop! And that's the sound of the police.

"Shit!" she cursed as she pulled over to the curb.

She had, had a bad feeling about it from the beginning, but she was so strung out over Tariq, she let him talk her into it.

"But Tariq, what if they're watching the car, just to see who comes for it?" she reasoned with him.

"For what? It's a million cars at McDonald's. Don't worry about it, baby, just go get it," he told her, giving her the keys and a kiss.

She accepted both.

Now her worst fear had become a reality. Her hands literally shook on the steering wheel as the police approached.

"License and registration, ma'am," the cop requested.

Even though it was nighttime and her face was hidden in the shadows, she felt like he could see the fear in her eyes.

"Is there a problem, officer?" she asked, struggling to keep the quiver from her voice.

"Actually there is. There was an incident here earlier, and we believe the driver of this vehicle was involved," he told her.

"I–I'm just . . . uh . . . doing a favor for a friend."

"I'm going have to ask you to turn off the car and step out of the vehicle, ma'am."

"I don't know about any incident," she protested weakly.

"I understand. Please turn off the car and step out of the vehicle, please, ma'am."

She did as she was told.

*****

The room was cold and sterile. No windows, just cinder blocks painted a dull gray. The vent blew cold air in a steady stream. The room felt like it was 40 degrees. She didn't know how long she had been sitting there, but she felt like it had been over an hour. She was scared and nervous and the longer she sat there, the worse her mind made it seem. But that's what the police wanted—for her to stew.

A female detective finally came in. Melissa Mulligan, a dirty blonde who resembled Angelina Jolie with her full lips and cattish eyes. She was all business as she opened a manila folder full of pictures and slid them in front of her. She looked at them and recoiled in horror.

The pictures were of three men dead at the scene in McDonald's. She had never seen dead people before, so to see their heads blown off, and one man with his eyes still open and blood everywhere, she almost lost it. If she had, had anything on her stomach, she would've thrown it up.

"Oh my God!" she gasped, covering her mouth.

"Look at them again."

"I don't—I've seen enough."

"Look. Again!" Melissa gritted.

"Why? I've seen—"

"No! Look!" Melissa ranted, holding one of the pictures up in her face. "Look again and again until it's etched in your brain! I want you to see what you've done!"

Her eyes swelled with fear. "Me? I didn't do that!"

"Bullshit!"

"No!"

"Bull. Shit! The person driving the Maserati did this. We've got several eye witnesses. You were picked up driving the Maserati, therefore you did it!" Melissa reasoned. She knew full well the suspect didn't have it in her to kill, but she was softening her up for the kill.

"I was only doing a favor for a friend!" she cried.

"Some friend. Because now you're going down for murder one." Melissa smiled evilly. She gathered up the photos, put them back in the folder, and started to get up.

"Tariq Acevedo!" she blurted.

Melissa sat back down. "We know whose car it is, and we're also well aware of who Tariq Acevedo is. The question is, do you know who he is?"

She wiped her tears. "He—he's my boyfriend."

Silly, misguided girl. Melissa looked amused, but replied, "Go on."

"He–he told me to pick up his car at McDonald's." She shook her head. "But I saw on the news wh-what had happened."

"So you knowingly became an accomplice to murder one? Wow, the sex must really be good," Melissa quipped.

"I didn't know!" she sobbed.

"What? What was going on and that you really are this stupid?"

She didn't answer, she just cried.

"But I can help you . . . if you help me."

She looked up at Melissa. "How?"

Who's dumber? Her for believing me, or Tariq for trusting she wouldn't? Melissa joked.

"Like I said, we know who Tariq is. What we don't know, we could use some help finding out."

She traced a circle absentmindedly on the table, looking at Melissa from under her eyelids. "I don't know nothin' about the murders."

Melissa smiled and leaned into the conversation. "The murders don't matter. We know there's been bad blood between the Rosario Brothers and the Acevedo family, and Tariq and Antonio are both itching for a war. All I'm asking you to do is keep in touch. Let me know what you know, what you think you know, and why. Simple," Melissa explained.

She looked at her. "I can do that!"

Melissa nodded. "Smart girl." She slid her card across the table. "That's my number. And I'll be expecting a call at least once a week."

She took the card, put it in her pocket, then replied, "Can I go now?"

Melissa stood up and opened the door. "See you soon."

Chapter 6

Lethal Weapon

Look at this shit, yo. It's like she fuckin' taunting you," Bas hissed, shaking his head. His handsome face and ballplayer height made everyone take at least a lengthy single glance. His thick eyebrows amplified his light skin and dark brown eyes.

Dressed in dark suits, he and Santiago stood in back of the Hilton Hotel ballroom where Operation Outreach, Santiago's charity for youth education was having its annual banquet. Some of the city's richest and most influential people had come to donate money for the cause. This was the city's powerful inner circle, the circle Santiago wanted to join, so he was being most charming. But Mel was pushing it and she knew it. Throughout the night, she was always the first to laugh at Alex's comments, first to second Alex's opinion. Her demeanor wasn't flirtatious to the point the people around her noticed, but it was like a dog's whistle to Santiago's already heightened sense of her rhythm.

He sipped his drink and observed Mel and Alex, watching the way she would laugh and lightly touch his arm at the same time. It was a wonder the liquor didn't start boiling in Santiago's glass; he was so hot.

"What did you find out?" Santiago questioned.

"Alex is definitely making moves in ATL, and not only that, here in the city, too. He's got a core crew of maybe nine strong that's loyal to him. So if we move on him, we most definitely gonna have to move on them," Bas replied.

"I want you to . . . to follow Mel. The next time Alex and Mel meet will be their last," Santiago vowed through clenched teeth.

"I got you, Big Brah. In the meantime I'll see about takin' care of his crew," Bas suggested.

Santiago looked at Bas. "Tell me something, yo . . . you think he had anything to do with the hit on Tariq?"

Bas rubbed his hairless chin, then replied, "Honestly yo, I can't say. I mean, he was there, and the way Tariq explained it, he was outside the restaurant when the nigguhs came in, so I can see the setup. But that don't mean it was his setup, feel me?" He pinched his broad nose slightly.

"Indeed," Santiago responded.

"Let's not jump to conclusions if we don't have to. It'll all come to the light anyway," Bas reasoned.

Santiago heard Bas's words, but his attention was on Mel as she approached. He hated the fact that no matter how incensed he was, she still turned him on like no other woman ever had. She looked exquisite in her off the shoulder Notte gown by Marchesa Fontaine, and her delectable toes played peek-a-boo in Valentino Couture bow lace pumps. Mel's natural walk was so sultry, it bordered on nasty and her smirk said she knew it. Their eyes met as she approached, and Santiago felt a sense of self-analysis forming in the back of his mind. He wondered had he treated her better over the years, would she still have cheated? If he hadn't made her put up with all the other chicks, the affairs, and even the child on the side, would he still be standing here, so sick realizing he had the baddest female in the world and he had blown it.

Mel walked up.

"What's up, Mel? How you?" Bas greeted her.

She ignored him and told Santiago, "I'm ready to leave."

"Yeah . . . I bet you are," he replied.

Her gaze told him she knew he wasn't talking about the party.

As Santiago walked behind her, hypnotized by the sway in her hips, his mind floated back to better times, better days, before their marriage ship began to sink.

Fifteen years ago . . .

Although he was only eighteen, Santiago had already had so many women that he had literally lost count. But that was to be expected. He was young, rich, and fine. Carlos had given him the power to run reckless in the city, and Santiago didn't waste the opportunity. His murder game was fierce, but with the ladies, his dick game was his lethal weapon.

Until he saw Mel naked for the first time.

From the moment he laid eyes on her in that Chinese restaurant, he knew she was the goddamn truth. But three days later, when he had wined and dined her out of her panties, her beauty damned near stopped his heart.

"You like what you see?" She smiled seductively as she strutted across the hotel room to him.

"Hell yeah!" he croaked, throat dry from wanton desire. His eyes took in every inch of her. From her tiny ballerina-like feet that made him want to lick toes for the first time in his life, to her shapely legs that got thicker and juicier until they blossomed out to her coke bottle hips, slight pouch of a stomach that only made the pertness of her chocolate chip-nippled C-cups even more tantalizing. She was the perfect package and the hardness of his dick said it all.

"So do I," she replied, gripping his dick through his jeans and sucking on his bottom lip.

Mel pulled his dick out of his jeans and dropped down, getting her eagle on. She ran the head of his dick around her mouth and on her cheeks before taking the head in her mouth while fondling his nuts.

"Ssssss," Santiago hissed, his toes curling in his gators.

She took his dick out of her mouth. "You like that, daddy? Tell me you like that," Mel cooed.

"I love it!" he groaned.

She smiled and devoured him whole, deep throating all nine inches. Santiago was in heaven. He felt like he was hitting the jackpot, not knowing she had done this hundreds, if not thousands of times. For every chick he had, she had been had twice as many times. But this time was different for Mel because she truly wanted to please him. She wanted to prove you could turn a whore into a housewife.

Santiago could feel the surge of the coming explosion, so he pulled her to her feet, ordering her to, 'Turn around."

"Daddy gonna beat this pussy from the back?" She stood in a sexy pose.

As she bent over the bed, exposing her pretty brown mound, Santiago's dick jumped with anticipation. Mel reached back and spread her pussy lips, looking over her shoulder at him. "Fuck this hot pussy, daddy."

Santiago gripped the base of his dick like a guided missile and slid deep inside Mel's wet pussy.

"Ohhhhhh," she cooed, as his girth spread her wide. She loved when a man filled her up.

He grabbed her hips and began pulling her back into each thrust with a steady rhythm. The pussy felt like warm pudding, creamy and gushy, and the sex song trickling from her full lips was the sweetest he had ever heard.

"I'ma make this pussy all mine," he grunted, pumping her full of his dick.

"It's–It's already yours," she squealed.

"Tell me again!"

"It's yours, Daddy, it's yours! This pussy all yours!"

The words felt so good to his ears, he couldn't fight the surge of the nut rushing for release.

"Cum in this pussy, cum in this pussy," Mel urged, bucking against him with lustful vigor.

Their slapping skins sounded like applause as Santiago exploded, creaming her walls and making her cum right behind him. They collapsed on the side of the bed, the moment so intense, they were both out of breath.

"Damn, lil' mama, you tryin' to turn a nigguh out?" Santiago chuckled, his dick still rock hard, something that had never happened before. Mel definitely had him open.

She wasted no time climbing on top of him and riding him slow and steady, like she was massaging his dick with her pussy.

"I hope our baby has your eyes," Mel remarked, her voice a quiver from the sensation of his dick hitting her spot.

Santiago smirked. "You act like you in this for real."

"I let you into the tenderest place on earth."

"I know. I can feel it."

"Not here," she replied, looking in his eyes, taking his hand and putting it on her pussy. "Here—" she ended, placing his hand over her heart.

That was the moment Santiago fell in love with her. He pulled her close, kissed her forehead, and caressed her cheek.

"What's your story, ma?"

"I'm just a girl looking for someone to love and someone to love me. Someone that won't leave me or push me away," Mel replied, thinking of her parents, Miss Brooks, and how easy she chose Maria over her.

"Let me be that someone," Santiago offered.

A tear rolled down Mel's cheek, a result of that good dick deep inside her, those sweet words in her ear, and the warm feeling in her heart. "Don't start something you can't finish, Santiago. I refuse to be hurt again," she warned.

He kissed her gently and answered, "I will never hurt you. I promise."

She kissed him back, then rode him until the sun came up.

At first, Santiago made Mel's life like a fairy tale. It wasn't only him buying her everything she wanted, but he also gave her what was most valuable. His time. They were inseparable. He told her his dreams. She told him her fears, even about her past. It only made him want to protect her more, which became evident one night at a club . . .

The Vortex was the hottest club in the city and Carlos was its secret owner, therefore, Santiago and his crew had free reign. They may as well have named it Santiago's because that's how he carried it, like he owned the place.

Santiago had just copped his first Bentley, and you couldn't tell him nothing. It was cocaine white with jet black interior, and his initials hand stitched into each headrest. He stepped out of it with Mel on his arm, killing the game, making haters so sick and bitches so wet. His team brought up the rear and trailed him like a long ass five o'clock shadow.

Mel loved to dance. So as soon as they hit the club, she led him straight to the dance floor. They danced a few songs until Santiago had to half drag her off to VIP.

"One more song, daddy. Please! I promise I'll be a bad girl when we get home tonight," she pouted like a spoiled sexpot.

Santiago chuckled. "You're gonna be that anyway. Come on, I have to meet somebody. Then I'll dance with you."

As soon as they hit VIP, everybody gave him dap and kisses because everybody loved a star, and Santiago was definitely the star in the movie. He approached their usual table where Alex and Bas were holding court with three dreaded Jamaicans.

Once Santiago and Mel sat down, Bas made the introductions.

"Yo, big bro, this is the dread I was tellin' you about. Ras, this is my main man Santiago."

Santiago and Ras shook hands.

"Respect my yout'. Me 'ere good things 'bout yah."

Santiago nodded.

Ras was an older dread who had the exotic smoke game on smash. They were looking to make major moves with Santiago and his crew until . . .

"Pardon me, star, but me and your uncle go back a long way," Ras remarked, adding, "and I see things 'ave prospered. Respect, mon'. Jah bless."

As soon as he said the words, Mel's whole body froze. She had been feeling a crazy vibe ever since she sat down. Like her body just started itching. She had gone to the bathroom three times during the course of their conversation. She had no reason to connect it to Ras's presence, because she had long ago blacked out the gory details of the night her parents were killed. All she remembered was that they had been murdered, but once he said those two words, "Jah bless," the two words that had haunted her dreams, her subconscious, her soul, it all came flooding back in a rush so strong that it at first froze her, then it made her throw up all over the floor.

"Goddamn! Baby, you okay?" Santiago exclaimed, narrowly avoiding being vomited on.

"I have to go," she mumbled, all but running from the booth.

"Yo, my bad, but I'ma have to get back at you."

"No problem, star! 'Andle your business," Ras replied, but in the back of his mind, he felt the negative energy.

Throughout the night, he had snuck a glance at Mel. At first it was because of her beauty, then he realized she was Jamaican, because he was good at spotting his people. But with every stolen glance, something told him he knew her. There was no way to connect Mel to that night because he had killed hundreds of people, so one didn't stand out. Besides, she had been a scrawny child covered in blood, not a drop dead gorgeous woman covered in bling. When she left he thought nothing else of it.

Meanwhile outside, Santiago finally caught up with Mel. "Mel!"

"No!"

He grabbed her arm, but she jerked away. "I have to go!"

"Mel!" he barked, seizing her firmly by both arms and looking into her eyes.

At first, her eyes were glazed over, as if she was there physically but not mentally. The look scared him, so he shook her.

"Mel! Talk to me, baby! What's wrong!"

She finally looked at him, and came to her senses. As soon as she did, she broke down in his arms crying. "Oh my God! Oh my God!" she sobbed into his chest. Her whole body was shivering. He held her tight. "Mel, what's wrong?"

"Its . . . It's him, it's him!"

"Him who?"

"Him! The man who killed my parents!"

She had told Santiago the story, but never the details. Now, she told him everything, about the heat, the machetes, the blood and her mother's last words.

"She said 'Melanie, I love you.' Oh my God! I remember now!" she cried.

Santiago was so hot he could've pushed the nuclear button on the whole world and watched it explode all around them as he held her tight. But he did one better. He pushed the button on Ras.

His jaw tightened as he held her out at arms' length and handed her the car keys.

"Go home. Go to sleep, and when you open your eyes, the man who caused you all this pain will no longer exist," he explained, then headed back toward the club.

At first, Mel hesitated. Then she turned and said, "Santiago."

He stopped and turned to her.

"I . . . I want to go with you."

Santiago knew what she was asking, but murder was a serious thing. He held out his hand, and she took it. Then they both went inside.

Something inside Ras told him that a certain malevolence dwelled in the way Santiago was approaching him, but he was tripped up by his own ego, thinking he would always be predator and not prey. But once he saw Santiago pull out his gun and put it so close to his face the barrel grazed his nose, he realized even predators can be hunted.

Bas and Alex didn't know what was going on, but once they saw Santiago pull his gun, they pulled theirs without hesitating and pointed at the other two dreads.

"Wha gwan?" Ras asked with his hands and eyebrows raised.

"You remember my lady from anywhere?" Santiago asked calmly but intently.

A smirk crept across his face. His instincts hadn't failed him. He just failed to pay attention. "'Er face is familiar," he replied.

"Look her in the eyes and apologize for livin'," Santiago hissed.

Ras knew right then he was a dead man, but he took it in stride. He had watched too many men die not to be prepared for it himself.

He turned to Mel, nodded and said, "Jah bless."

A chill went up her spine, but instead of vomit, her fear and rage came up as she spat dead in his face.

Boom! Boom!

Santiago put two in Ras's face and had him bleeding watermelon chunks.

Boom! Boom!

Bas and Alex followed in quick succession with single shots to the other dreads' foreheads, blowing their brains all over the people in the booth behind them.

The music stopped and people stared in Santiago's direction in shock. He looked around.

"What's the matter? You see anything strange, huh? Do you?" he asked, gun in hand, looking at various people.

One by one they dropped their heads.

"Turn the music back on!" he yelled to the deejay.

The music started back up and Santiago turned to Bas. "Clean up this mess," he ordered, then he took Mel's hand and casually headed for the door.

From that moment on, the streets knew young Santiago was no joke. It was also the moment Mel knew that Santiago's love for her was so strong that he would kill for her, but it would be years before she found out that, that same love would turn out to be a double-edged sword.

Once Tariq was born, things began to go downhill. Throughout their relationship, Santiago always had side chicks that Mel more or less knew about. She put up with it, knowing that most men had more than one woman, especially men in the game. But Santiago always took care of home in every way, so she allowed it space only in the back of her mind. Nevertheless, like the old adage goes: "Nothing lasts forever."

Santiago's 23rd birthday altered everything about his relationship with Mel. The party was held on a yacht that cruised the city's harbor while the party went on until the break of day. Everybody that was anybody in the game was there.

Mel was having a ball. She loved the respect and attention that came with being Santiago's wife. If he was the king, then she most definitely was the queen, and she carried herself as such. She could feel the envy and hate in almost every woman's eyes in attendance, and she took it as confirmation that she was definitely that bad bitch. Her favorite song by Mary J. Blige came on, and she looked around for Santiago to no avail. She realized she hadn't seen him in a while, so she set out to find him. When she did, she didn't like what she found.

"That's right, bitch! Just like that. Eat all of Daddy's dick," Santiago grunted. He gripped the back of the head of some red bone with red hair, who was on her knees, deep-throating Santiago.

They were in the rear of the boat, supposedly out of sight, yet not hard to find. That's how Mel walked up on them and got sick at the sight.

"Santiago!" she gasped, one hand flew to her mouth, the other to her stomach. She'd expected Santiago to react with surprise, to stutter, to do something other than what he did.

He simply smiled.

The girl stopped sucking his dick and began to pull back, but he gripped her head and pushed it back in position.

"Did I tell you to stop?" he asked the chick, then looked up at Mel. "I'm busy right now."

Mel was stuck. Tears streamed down her face. "How could you do this to me?" she cried.

"Ma, don't act so surprised. This is what I do. So either play your position, or if you can't hang . . ." He shrugged and let his voice trail off, leaving the implication hanging in mid-air.

Shaking her head and crying, Mel backed away. She took one last look, then turned and ran off, crashing smack dab into Bas.

"Mel, you okay?"

She pushed past him and ran off. Bas headed in the direction she had just come from. When he saw Santiago, he knew why she was crying. He shook his head and turned away, waiting for Santiago on the other side of the wall.

Several moments later, Santiago and the chick emerged from the shadows. She was patting her hair back in the place while Santiago buttoned his pants. He patted her on the ass with a wink and sent her on her way. He approached Bas, who was leaning on the rail looking out at the reflection of the moon on the water.

"You think that's wise?" Bas questioned.

"What? Mel? She'll be all right," Santiago replied dismissively.

Bas looked at him. "Big Brah, how you carry your marriage is on you, but the pen full wit' nigguhs who turned they own bitch against em'. Feel me?"

"No doubt . . . but what's on your mind?"

"I just got word, yo. Uncle Carlos is dead. They killed him."

Chapter 7

Family and Like Family

Cookie giggled as Tariq sniffed coke off the inside of her thigh, but her giggles turned to moans of passion when his lips wrapped around her clit. "Ooohh, baby, you know I loooovvve that," she gushed.

Tariq cocked her legs up over his shoulders and cupped his hands under her ass. He ran his tongue around the length of her pussy, all the way to her asshole. Cookie squirmed and squealed with pleasure and delight.

The only thing Tariq liked better than killing was fucking and sniffing coke. Both gave him a rush that made him feel totally alive. The coke kept him as hard as a roll of quarters, giving him the ability to fuck all night.

Pushing her legs back until her toes touched the headboard, Tariq slid up balls deep in her already sloppy wet pussy and beat it like they had beef. Cookie couldn't do anything but thrash her head from side to side, clawing at the sheets while he gave her a dicking down that always made her pussy squirt upon climax.

"Ta–Ta–Tariq, oh fuck, Tariq! That's my spot!" she moaned.

Tariq began grinding that spot relentlessly, until her legs began to twitch and tremble.

"Damn this pussy good," he grunted, loving the tightness of Cookie's walls.

"I'm squirting!" she squealed, releasing her juices hard and direct.

Tariq kept stroking, unable to cum because of the coke stimulating his veins and pumping his heart a mile a minute.

After her third orgasm, Cookie begged him to slow down, looking over her shoulder at him. Unmerciful, he continued pounding her from the back.

"No more, daddy. No more!"

Tariq reluctantly slowed as Cookie collapsed on the bed.

"You tryin' to kill a bitch or something," she cracked, picking up the blunt in the ashtray and lighting it. "Here, you need to mellow out."

Tariq sniffed the air. "Why this shit smell funny?"

Cookie shrugged and hit the blunt. "It's got coke in it."

"Coke? Oh hell no! I ain't smoking that shit," he replied, handing her back the blunt.

"Boy. It ain't but the same shit you snortin'," she reminded him, turning the blunt around. "Here, I'ma blow you a gun."

"Naw, I'm good."

She blew the smoke anyway. He turned his head, but he couldn't lie though, the smell of the burning coke and the exotic smelled good together.

"Come on, baby, just one time," she urged with a puff. "I'll let you beat it 'til it's sore."

Tariq looked at her. "One time?"

"One time."

"A'ight . . . one time," were his famous last words.

She blew the smoke into his mouth and he inhaled the coke–laced blunt. The mellow effect of the exotic and the tingling sizzle of the coke blended well and went straight to his brain, lighting up his neurons like Forty-Second Street in '89. If sniffing coke was a rush, then smoking it was a blast . . .

A blast . . .

"Bangin', ain't it?" She smirked, reading his expression.

Before he could answer, someone rang his doorbell. He knew who it was, so he didn't hesitate to throw on his pants and sneakers.

"Hurry back," Cookie cooed, spreading her legs and opening her pussy lips. "She was ready to be punished."

Tariq walked down the hall to the door, feeling like he was floating. "Yo," he said when he got to the door.

"You already know," Bas replied.

Tariq opened the door and Bass stepped in. "I thought you said an hour, unc?"

Bas chuckled. "Nigguh, it's been an hour. Your girl must be over here."

"She think she my girl. My girls are in my pocket," Tariq shot back.

They both laughed.

"I know that's right," Bas remarked. He smelled the weed and the coke but didn't say anything. "You ready?"

"Yeah, but yo, I still don't understand," Tariq replied.

Bas nodded. "I know it's hard to wrap your head around it, but it is what it is, yo. It's a dirty game."

"Shit, I know that, but goddamn . . . Murk, B, and Smoke? They some of Pop's most loyal soldiers." Tariq shook his head.

Bas scowled. "Naw nephew, *I'm* one of your father's most loyal soldiers. You one of your father's most loyal soldiers. That's who we count on, feel me? That's why we gonna handle it."

"And Alex, you can't forget, unc," Tariq added.

Bas smiled. "Naw . . . can't forget Alex." He knew Santiago hadn't told Tariq the situation, so neither did he, nor did he tell him where he had just come from. Following his mother.

Bas had trailed her from the hair salon, her favorite alibi. She snaked through traffic, and he stayed right behind her. She headed straight to the Holiday Inn hotel on the outskirts of town. She parked. He parked around the building. As soon as she entered the room, he made the call.

"Unc, you hear me?" Tariq questioned.

Bas came back to the present. "Yeah."

"I said, why don't we wait 'til Alex get back from ATL?"

Bas smiled. "Your father doesn't want Alex to . . . get his hands dirty on this one, so it's only me and you. That is, unless you scared," Bas cracked, throwing a playful jab at Tariq.

"Fuck no! It's just crazy, yo. Them nigguhs like family."

Bas put his hand around his neck and replied, "Family and like family are two different things. Never mistake the two, nephew, because sometimes love ain't enough." Bas schooled him.

Tariq nodded. "No doubt."

"A'ight, go get dressed. Let's go handle our biz."

Chapter 8

Suspicion

W"here did you get this weed from? This is banging!" Asia giggled, passing the blunt to Eva.

They were in Asia's room smoking a blunt. Asia was Eva's best friend. They had been tight since third grade. Both were beautiful and smart. Asia resembled a young Lisa Bonet from her *Cosby Show* years, braces and all.

"I stole it from Tariq's stash. He gonna kill me when he find out," Eva remarked, inhaling the exotic.

"Tell him to kill me instead," Asia said, rolling her hips.

"Sssss, you still have a crush on Tariq? That's so nasty!"

"Trust, you ain't seen nasty yet!"

Eva rolled her eyes. "Changing the subject . . . tell me something, do you think it's crazy to talk to yourself?"

"As long as you don't answer." Asia shrugged.

"I know, but what if answers just like pop in your head without you thinking them?" Eva probed.

Asia took the blunt. "Then yeah, you're probably loony."

Eva pushed her playfully. "Shut up, I'm not loony."

"You asked." Asia laughed.

"No, for real, for real, I'm having crazy dreams, yo, like . . . crazy. It's like, how it feels like me, but it's not me, you know? Like . . . I don't know, I can't explain." Eva sighed, growing frustrated.

"Crazy like what?"

"Like I'm . . . or she's—the person in my dreams—is killing people and she likes it."

"Killing them on some Jason shit?"

"No, on some gangsta shit with guns," Eva answered.

The blunt was too small to hit again, so Asia put it out in the ashtray. "No offense, but you come from a family full of gangsters, maybe your dreams are trying to tell you something," Asia joked.

"I'm not like my family." Eva looked at her seriously.

"Relax, I was just kidding." Asia playfully muffed her.

Eva held her dead on gaze, which prompted Asia to make herself go cross-eyed. Eva chuckled.

"I'm sayin', yo, I'm not my family."

"I know. But on the real, doesn't it ever scare you? I mean, didn't you say they tried to kill Tariq? Like, that's not normal."

Pulling her knees to her chest, Eva wrapped her arms around her legs. "True. But, I never look at it like that. Whoever my father is in the street, he's just Daddy at home, you know?"

"Yeah but, what about the police? Don't you ever worry that they will kick in the door and you'll lose everything?"

Eva shrugged. "My father's been doing this a long, long time, and they haven't kicked in the door yet."

"Doesn't mean they won't."

"And why all this sudden interest in my family?" Eva asked in a light tone to take the sting out of any suspicion she couldn't help but feel.

"I just worry about you sometimes. You're my BFF, I'm supposed to," Asia replied.

Eva smiled warmly, but she couldn't shake the nagging feeling the conversation had given her.

Chapter 9

Clouded Vision

Tariq watched the group of men file into the warehouse, giving many of them pounds and gangsta hugs, knowing they wouldn't make it out alive. He looked from face to face with a deep sense of respect and a lump in his throat. There were seven in all, including dudes who had practically raised him, like, Murk, B, and Smoke. He couldn't believe they were plotting to move on his father, but like Santiago always told him, "Money and pussy are the two things that can make brothers enemies." As he looked around, he could see how right Santiago had been.

Bas entered the room carrying a fully automatic AK-47 over his shoulder like a bat. When he stepped in the circle of men, all side conversations stopped. He looked around from face to face. "We called y'all here for one thing and one thing only. To get to the bottom of who put the hit on my fuckin' nephew!"

The men looked around, confusion apparent on their faces.

"Yo, Bas, we want the same thing," Murk replied, "but we don't know no more than you."

Bas stepped up to Murk. "We? You feel like you can speak for every man in this room?"

"Nigguh, we all came up together. Hell yeah, I feel like that!" Murk answered without hesitation.

Bas looked at him with a smirk. "Unfortunately, I can't. The shit that went down at McDonald's had an inside man in on it, and the only ones it could be is in this room!" Bas' voice boomed.

Smoke shook his head. "Wait, wait, you mean you feel like one of us set Tariq up?"

"Naw, Smoke, I don't feel like it. I, I know it. One man in here is workin' for the Rosario Brothers!" Bas accused.

Nervous chatter filled the room. Tariq could feel the tension, so he pulled his gun out and clicked off the safety.

"Yo, Tariq, you feel like that too?" Murk questioned, eyeing the gun now in Tariq's hand.

"All I know is a muhfucka tried to kill me, and I know it couldn't have happened if a muhfucka ain't know where I was 'posed to be," Tariq answered.

A phone rang and one dude went to reach for it. Bas snatched the AK-47 off his shoulder and aimed. "Naw, playboy, let it ring. You can call back."

The dude did exactly that.

"Now . . . I'm gonna ask one time . . . Who the fuck turned on us?" Bas bassed, waving the gun.

Smoke knew right then what was going on. None of them would leave the room alive.

"Ay yo, Bas, you a fuckin' *snake*," Smoke sneered.

"Then you should've seen this coming!" Bas blasted back.

Brrrrrrrrppppp! Brrrrrrrpppppp!

The AK-47 mowed them down like helpless blades of grass. Two dudes thought they had time to pull their guns, but Tariq proved them wrong.

Boc! Boc! Boc!

Tariq shot one in the throat and the heart, killing him instantly. The other took one to the brain that left him slumped and twitching. The whole room smelled like gun smoke. Tariq and Bas scanned the bodies, looking for any signs of life.

Boc! Boc! went their guns if they found anyone breathing.

Tariq came to Smoke who was choking on his own blood. Their eyes met.

"You're . . . you're . . . ech," Smoke stuttered, his words garbled and mangled.

Tariq raised the gun and put one in his dome. In his heart it was a mercy killing because he didn't want Smoke to suffer any more than he had to.

He and Bas surveyed their work.

"Goddamn shame, yo," Bas said, shaking his head. "Every one of these nigguhs were good soldiers. But greed clouded their vision," he remarked and looked at Tariq intently. "Never forget this lesson, nephew. Never forget . . . family comes first."

Tariq nodded and took one last look at the dead men.

"Yo . . . go get the gas out the trunk," Bas told him.

Tariq headed outside with a guilty heart. He'd just committed a great evil, although in his mind he felt it was a necessary evil. For some reason he couldn't get his heart and mind to agree. Therefore, he needed to smoke.

Three hours later, Tariq parked the car and texted: *Come out.*

He then put the lighter to the tip of his blunt and puffed it to full flame and savored the taste as it engulfed his system. He was beginning to love the coke-laced blunt Cookie had turned him on to. It was mellow but still intense, an addictive combination. He needed it because he couldn't get the very scene out of his mind. He had never known this part of the game where those closest to you turn on you. He hoped to never see it again.

The more he smoked, the less he thought of it. The smoke had him in a zone. He almost didn't see her approach the car. The suddenness of the interior light coming in as she got in startled him.

"Damn, Asia . . . fuck you do? Tiptoe?" Tariq growled.

"Didn't you tell me to come out?" she said with a hint of young sass in her tone.

Tariq smiled. Asia was his young girl that he kept in the cut. No one knew about her, not even Eva.

"You know your sister is spending the night, right?" Asia informed him.

She had been lying in the bed when his text came through. She checked on Eva, but she was knocked out. Before heading out to meet him, Asia hopped up and took off her panties because she knew that's how Tariq liked it.

"She sleep?" he asked.

"Yeah, but what if she wasn't?" Asia reminded him.

He smiled and caressed her cheek. "Don't worry about it."

Tariq put his hand on the back of her neck and pulled her face into his lap, unbuckling his pants at the same time. Asia wasted no time pulling his dick out and sliding it in her mouth. Tariq's toes curled in his sneakers. He had taught her well, he thought.

Asia ran her tongue along the length of his dick until she reached his balls and took them in her mouth one at a time.

"Ssssss." He sucked in a breath and inhaled the blunt at the same time.

She then took him in her mouth and began sucking his dick with no hands, twisting her neck, giving him that neck action he loved.

"Goddamn, ma! You gonna make me cum down your throat. Get in the backseat," Tariq told her.

Asia climbed over the seat, pulling her nightgown over her head to reveal she was butt naked underneath. She lay on her back and cocked her legs wide open, one on the back of the driver's seat and one in the back window.

Tariq slid inside her hot, wet, young pussy, making her wrap her legs around his waist. "Oooh baby, I missed you," she cooed, squeezing him tight.

"Damn this pussy tight," Tariq grunted.

"Yessss, and it's all yours, baby," Asia moaned.

Tariq cocked her legs back and began to pile drive that pussy, something he knew drove Asia crazy.

"Ohh fuck! Yes, beat this pussy!"

"You like that?"

"I love it!"

He was banging her so hard the whole car was rocking, the windows were fogged, and the car smelled like Asia's sweetness.

"Take all this dick!" Tariq bassed, feeling that familiar stirring building in his stomach.

Sensing it in his strokes, she urged him on. "Cum in my pussy, cum for meeeee!" she squealed, feeling an explosion of her own.

They came together then lay in each other's arms. When Asia got her breath back, she began softly kissing along his neck.

"Don't make me wait so long next time," Asia remarked softly, giving his dick a squeeze with her pussy muscles.

"Ma, you already know I live a crazy life," Tariq replied.

"If you ain't careful, you're gonna lose it," she shot back with concern in her eyes.

Tariq pulled out of her and sat up with a sigh. "Believe me, Asia, I'm good."

Asia sat up and got on his lap. "Tariq, this is me you are talking to. Remember, I'm the one who picked up the car for you, so I saw what happened," she reminded him.

He shrugged it off and relit the blunt. "Yeah, I've been meaning to ask you. You ain't have no problems?"

"No," Asia lied, keeping her poker face. She quickly changed the subject by grabbing the blunt out of his mouth. "What, you gonna smoke it all, greedy?" She giggled.

She hit the blunt, then frowned. "It tastes funny."

Tariq smiled. "It's some new shit. You like it?"

She hit it again, harder and longer, not knowing the coke was working its way into her system. "Yeah, it feels . . . cool," she remarked, hitting it again. She blew out the smoke and her whole body felt open, making her horny all over again. "I want to be your ride or die chick," Asia said, grinding on his dick.

"I bet you do." He chuckled.

"I'm serious, Tariq. I can handle it. I took care of your car, didn't I?"

Tariq hit the blunt and thought about it. She was young, but that only meant he could mold her. Plus she wasn't hood, so he knew she could make moves the average ghetto chick couldn't. What he didn't know was she was already riding for somebody.

The police.

"We'll see," he answered, handing her the blunt.

As she hit the blunt, he reached down and slid his half hard dick back in her pussy.

"I promise, baby . . . I'll play my position," she cooed, leaving out the part that the detective had already given her a position.

Tasha Macklin

Chapter 10

Food for Thought

I t's done."

"Good. What about the rest?"

"As soon as Alex gets back, I'll send a team down ATL to handle it."

Pause.

"What about the other thing?"

"I think they're planning on meeting up Saturday."

Santiago chuckled and gulped his drink as he gazed out his study window at the pool area. Mel was in a yellow two-piece bikini looking chocolate and delicious, headphones on her head, oblivious to Santiago's studied gaze.

"What's so funny?" Bas asked.

Santiago looked away from the window and at Bas.

"That's the week of my birthday."

"I didn't want to point that out."

"She really tryin' to rub it in, huh?" Santiago smirked to himself as he sat down behind his desk and finished his drink.

Bas sighed. "Big Brah, you don't have to do this, okay? Once all is taken care of, Alex won't have a team. He'll be toothless."

"What are you suggesting, Bas? Let him live?"

Bas sat down on the opposite side of the desk. "I just know how hard it is for you. Alex is your own blood."

"Which makes it even easier," Santiago shot back smoothly. "If he can betray me so easily, why would it be any harder for me?"

Bas nodded, understanding his point. "What about her?"

"What about her?" Santiago replied with the same words, but a different emphasis. "I don't know."

"And if you . . . what would you tell Eva and Tariq?" Bas probed.

Santiago rose from his chair and went and poured himself another drink. This time a double. "Like I said, I don't know."

"I told you a long time ago, many nigguhs downfall was a woman, and being one hunnid, you put her through a lot. Sometimes a woman deserves the benefit of a doubt, too," Bas schooled him.

Santiago chuckled. "Since when did you become an expert on women, player?" Santiago quipped, referring to the fact that Bas always vowed to stay single.

A hardy laugh exploded from Bas and he stood up. "Just some food for thought, Big Brah."

After the laughter subsided, Santiago said, "I don't want anybody else knowing about this. It's between me and you."

Bas nodded. "I figured that, yo. Don't worry, it is."

Bas walked out, leaving Santiago to contemplate his words of wisdom. Soon, those reflective questions arose. *What about Mel? Would she be his downfall?* His conscience sent him travelling back in time.

Ten years ago, Santiago woke up with a gun on his nose. His sleepy eyes focused instantly. He had been out all night partying in Vegas with Bas, Alex, and a bunch of chicks. They had rented a private plane on a whim for the Mayweather fight. He had just gotten in twenty minutes earlier and fell out in his clothes from exhaustion and drunkenness. When he felt the gun on his nose, he thought it was over. Finally, the Rosario Brothers had caught him slipping.

But it was Mel.

She pretended to be asleep when he lay across their king-sized bed smelling like pussy and perfume, and right then she decided she wouldn't take anymore.

The sound of the cocking hammer awoke Santiago, and once he did, the kiss of steel to his nose let him know this was no dream.

Mel grabbed at him through mascara-streaked eyes. "I'm tired of your shit, Santiago! I'm tired of you disrespecting me, comin' home smellin' like the next bitch and lyin' in my bed," she ranted, her voice occasionally choked with sobs.

Santiago's temper boiled beneath the surface like a volcano destined to erupt, but her finger was on the trigger, and he knew she was on edge. But he didn't seek to placate her by sweet-talking the gun out of her hand. His ego wouldn't let him. Instead, he came at her a different way.

Santiago's gaze met with Mel's tormented eyes. "Then shoot! . . . Go ahead and pull the trigger. Then what? Huh?"

"Then I'll . . . be . . . free of . . . your . . . bullshit!" she spat in a measured tone, gripping the gun tighter as if preparing to shoot.

"And our kids will be bastards," he reminded her. "Tariq . . . Eva, all alone in this cold world. I'll be dead and you'll be in jail and they'll be in some foster home like you grew up in. You want that for them? Then pull the trigger and do to them what them Jamaicans did to you."

His last words struck her like a punch in the gut, knocking the wind from her, as her words caught in her throat.

She gasped. "H-h-how could you say that to me?"

"How could you put a gun in my fuckin' face!" Santiago shot right back with a sneer. He knew it was a low blow, but he knew his wife well enough to know the effect it would have on her.

She kept the gun in his face, but now it trembled with uncertainty. "You . . . son of a bitch!" she spat in a desperate whisper.

"Mommy, I want some water," a young Eva said from the hallway. She stood in the door in her nightgown and pigtails, rubbing the sleep from her eyes.

"I'll get you some water, baby," Santiago answered in a soothing tone, never taking his eyes off Mel, then added, "Are you gonna let me get the baby some water, or are you gonna kill me?"

The gun remained aimed, but it was no longer a threat. Santiago slid his legs from under Mel one at a time, then got off the bed. He picked Eva up and kissed her cheek, glancing at Mel with a mocking smirk. In seconds, he made his way down the hall.

As soon as he disappeared, Mel broke down in body-wracking sobs. She fell to the bed, gun still in hand, crying her eyes out. That morning she decided that one day she would make Santiago pay for the way he mistreated her. It was a vow that she had no intention of breaking.

A black Montblanc pen rolled off the desk onto the hardwood floor, bringing Santiago back to the present. He cast a final glance at Mel outside swimming laps in the pool. Santiago had always been a thinker, a strategist. Knowing he had leverage to keep Mel in her position allowed him to conduct himself as usual. That 'gun to the nose' situation had been placed under lock and key years ago, and even now he put the memory back where it rightfully belonged. Mel could never hurt him in any real way. But without even giving it much thought, he knew he could destroy her a million times over. The odds undeniably pointed in his favor.

Chapter 11

A War on Our Hands

Detective Melissa Mulligan bounded up the stairs of the precinct. Still in her running shoes, she power walked down the hall as she always did after her morning run. Her long blonde ponytail bounced with her every step as detectives and uniformed officers alike turned to watch her walk past.

When she reached her desk, another detective, James Lawrence, came over handing her a cup of coffee and a manila folder.

"Mornin' Mulligan," James greeted.

James was her partner. He was a cop's cop, tough but fair. He looked like Stephen A. Smith from ESPN, receding hairline and all.

"Mornin'," she returned, sipping her coffee. "Thanks."

She sat down at her desk and opened the folder. James looked from over her shoulder. What stared back at her were several mug shots, including those of Murk, B, and Smoke.

"Recognize any of them?" James asked, knowing she did.

"They're members of Santiago's inner circle," she answered.

"*Were,*" he corrected her. "Remember that warehouse blaze? All the burned bodies?"

Melissa looked at him, mouth agape. "You mean—"

He nodded. "Read the file, it's all there. I think we've got a war on our hands," he surmised.

"Or a major house cleaning."

"How so?"

She turned her chair to face him. "These guys were killers. Cold-blooded. There's no way the Rosarios could've gotten them all into one place and just gunned them down."

James stroked his goatee and contemplated her words. "So you're saying maybe Santiago believes they had something to do with the hit on Tariq?"

"Exactly."

"All of them?" he questioned skeptically.

Seeing the flaw in her argument, she hedged, "Kill 'em all and let God sort out his own, maybe. I don't know, but I'm willing to bet this wasn't a Rosario job."

"I'll agree with you there."

"Besides, I may not know, but I know someone who might."

"Who?"

She smirked as she dialed a number on her desk phone. After three rings she said, "Asia, we need to meet . . . Okay, text me as soon as you can get away."

Melissa hung up, looked at James and said, "Tariq's little girlfriend."

Chapter 12

Bloody Razor

Who was that?" Eva asked. She had just approached Asia, who had just ended a call on her cell phone and was leaving the school cafeteria.

Asia rolled her eyes and sucked her teeth playfully. "Nosy . . . really?" she said.

"I *know* you are not talkin'," Eva replied.

"Now, for real for real, it was this guy I met. He wants to meet after school," Asia lied, knowing it was the police she was really meeting.

"Well, do your thing. Don't let me stop you from bein' a slut," Eva joked.

Asia gave her the finger. "I'll call you."

"'Kay."

Asia went out the door while Eva headed for the bathroom. She didn't even see Kim and her sidekick

Trish coming from the other direction. Nor did she hear her enemy's threatening words. "Now see, if I was a dirty bitch I would go in there and beat her ass again just for GP," Kim remarked.

Trish giggled. "You are a dirty bitch."

"Shit, then you know what it is." Kim laughed and gave Trish a hi-five.

Eva stood at the sink when they came in. She saw them enter the bathroom while looking in the mirror. She and Kim's eyes met.

"I know you ain't think it was over," Kim huffed, taking off her earrings.

Eva turned. "Why don't you just let it go, okay? I said I was sorry."

"Naw, but you about to be though," Kim retorted as she and Trish approached.

Eva tried to make a break for the door, but Trish grabbed her in a choke hold and Kim punched her in the face.

"You think you so cute, don't you, bitch? Well, I got somethin' for your cute ass," Kim hissed. She pulled an orange box cutter from her pocket and dialed the blade to full height.

"No, please!" Eva begged, struggling against Trish's tight grip.

Her pleas and struggles only egged them on more. Kim wanted to be the prettiest girl in school, but Eva stood in her way. She was about to do something about that.

Eva stared at the blade, the sunlight glinting off its razor sharp edge as it neared her face, and she willed every inch of strength to break loose. Her survival instincts kicked in, and with it something else . . . something deeper . . . something she couldn't control.

"Get the fffuccck . . . away from me!" she barked and kicked out at the same time.

She caught Kim dead in the stomach, and Kim doubled over in agony. Eva quickly backed Trish up against the wall hard, slamming her back against a protruding metal rail.

"Ooofff!" Trish bellowed, breaking her grip on Eva.

Turning, Eva grabbed a fistful of Trish's hair, and brought her face down into her knee. Trish hit the floor, holding her nose and screaming, "My nose! My nose!" as blood squirted from it.

By the time she finished with Trish, Kim was struggling to get to her feet. A football kick to her face from Eva sent her crashing back down to the floor.

"This is what you bitches wanted, huh? Huh!" Eva cackled. Had either girl been able to hear her, they wouldn't have recognized her voice.

Eva snatched the razor from Kim's hand and started for Trish, who seeing the razor in her hand, got up like a motherfucka in the matrix. She pounced to her feet and raced out of the door before Eva took two steps. Turning back to Kim, Eva grabbed a handful of her long, silky hair and put the razor to it and started cutting— sawing out patches. Even in Kim's dazed state, she realized what was going on.

"Noooooo! My hair!" she screamed, putting a hand up to shield her hair. Eva sliced through that, too, damn near splitting her pinky to the bone.

"Aarrrggghhhh!" Kim hollered as blood flew everywhere.

"Don't holla now, bitch!" Eva laughed.

She began dragging Kim by the hair toward the stalls. Kim couldn't get any traction on the slippery linoleum floor to stop her. Once Eva got her in the stall, she beat her face against the hard porcelain commode until she knocked loose one of Kim's teeth. Eva proceeded to dunk her head in the toilet.

"Drink it or drown, bitch, drink it or drown," Eva growled, holding her head under. Kim's arms flailed wildly as she fought for her life, but Eva had all her weight on her neck keeping her under.

Suddenly, several security officers, Trish, and the principal burst into the bathroom.

"She's drowning her!" Trish snitched.

The security guards wrestled Kim loose just in time. A few more seconds and she would've drowned. Kim gasped for air, thrashing around like a fish.

"She tried–she tried to–to kill me!" she croaked.

"Eva!" the principal called out, but Eva gazed at someplace invisible to the others.

"Eva!" The second time he called, her whole body jumped and she looked at him.

"What? Where—" she stammered, looking around as if aware of her surroundings for the first time.

"Eva Acevedo, you are expelled from this school! Officers, please take Miss Acevedo home!" the principal commanded.

"Expelled? What did I—" Eva began to say, but when she looked around at all the blood, globs of hair, and bloody razor, she knew deep down that she was to blame.

Yet, had she said she hadn't done it, she wouldn't have been lying.

An hour later, Mel shut the door behind her and glared at Eva. After hearing the story the security guards told her, she didn't know what to think. "Expelled," she said, shaking her head.

"Ma, I don't want to go back to school. I–I want to do home schooling," Eva said.

"Like I got time to teach you," Mel guffawed, placing a hand on her hip.

"I can take courses online. Whatever, I just don't want to go back. Please," Eva pleaded. She still couldn't remember anything, but hearing the guards explain what she did sent a shiver down her spine.

"Truthfully, I don't care what you do, but I know this. I ain't got time for it right now."

Hearing her mother's indifference, Eva stormed from the room, mentally and emotionally bothered. What had become of her relationship with her mother? Why was it full of static? When she was younger they were so close. Eva just didn't understand.

Chapter 13

Closer to the Edge

Santiago would relive the moment over and over and over . . .

The moment Alex opened the door.

That night hard rains pelted the pavement, further clouding Santiago's vision. The Henny in his system took care of the rest. He had drunk half a bottle trying to waylay the gnawing feeling inside that he couldn't ignore. He thought it was just the love he had for Alex making one last appeal for mercy.

He was wrong.

"She just arrived, yo," Bas reported over the phone after following Melanie to Alex's home.

"I'm halfway there," Santiago replied, already en route.

The Chrome .45 sat in his lap like a trained pit bull. Silent, but deadly. The gleam caught his eye as he passed under a streetlight. His drunken mind began to wander. He thought of Mel and envisioned her sweet, chocolate body spread all over Alex's bed, one leg cocked up, her hands gripping the sheets while Alex stood over her, dick at full attention, ready to fulfill the need that Santiago could no longer fulfill. Every imagined kiss, moan, thrust, and bitten lip drove him closer and closer to the edge, and he was fully prepared to jump off.

He arrived at Alex's condo, spotted Bas posted up in the cut and approached him.

"You sure you want to do this?" Bas questioned.

"I go in alone," Santiago replied with a tight jaw.

Bas nodded. "I feel you, Big Brah. Handle your biz."

Santiago pulled his gun from his pants as he approached the door, keeping it down by his leg. He knocked. Waited. Heard the locks on the door disengaged.

Alex opened the door, and the first thing he did when he saw Santiago was smile.

He smiled . . .

That smile said it all to Santiago's jealous, enraged mind. The smile seemed to say "I win. You may be the boss, but I've got the prize. Your wife." That smile seemed to taunt him, challenge him. The smile alone was enough evidence to justify Santiago blowing Alex's brains out in the door. But he wanted to confront him, let him know he knew and listen to him beg for his life.

Until he saw Mel.

She came into view, visible over Alex's shoulders, clad only in one of Alex's shirts and shorts, heavily knotted at the waist. The sight was all it took to turn Santiago from a killer into a madman.

"You betrayed me!" Santiago bellowed and then raised the gun.

As soon as Alex saw the gun, he screamed, "Noooooo, Santiago, it's—"

Boc! Boc! Boc! Boc! Boc! Boc! Boc! Boc! Boc! Click!

Santiago unloaded all nine shots in Alex's face and brain, then stood over him to finish the job, exploding his gray matter all over the thick beige rug in the living room. Mel screamed uncontrollably. Santiago looked up at her with hell in his eyes. Lucky for her he had emptied his clip in Alex because there was no telling what he would've done to Mel.

"Oh my Goooood, Santiago! What have you done?" she cried.

Santiago backhanded her, and blood spewed from her mouth. He'd knocked her onto the couch.

"Cállate, puta! What have you done? You think you can betray me? *Me*! I'm like God to you, bitch. I know everything!" he bassed, drawing back to hit her again.

"Betray you? Santiago, what's wrong with you? Oh my God! I didn't betray you. We were planning your fucking surprise party!" Mel sobbed. "Look!"

Her words kept his hand suspended in mid-blow as her trembling hands held up the book on the table. The book was filled with games to be rented for a party. The rest of the table was covered in latex balloon samples in different colors bearing Santiago's initials as well as program samples embossed with the words "Happy Birthday, Santiago," in fancy script.

He staggered back, shaking his head, unable to square the reality being suddenly thrust upon him with the reality his thoughts had created for him. She handed Santiago an invitation, and he snatched it. "Fuckin' liar!" he roared.

"No!" she shot right back. "It's not a lie! He and I have been planning your party! Nothing more! The only reason I have on his clothes is because I spilled pasta sauce on my dress! Go look in the washer if you don't believe me!" Mel explained, taking the invitation from his hand and flinging it on the floor.

Just then, Bas came in.

"Big Brah, what you doin'? Somebody was bound to hear all those shots. We gotta go!"

Santiago looked around the room, his mind still reeling. *Birthday party?* his thought echoed.

"Santiago!" Bas said firmly.

"Take her to the car," he told Bas as he headed for the back.

"Where you go—"

"Take her and go!" Santiago bassed.

Bas didn't ask any more questions. He led Mel to his car.

Santiago went straight to Alex's pantry where he kept his washer and dryer. He snatched open the washer, and on first sight he felt vindicated because the washer looked empty. That is, until he put his hand inside and felt pure wet silk. His heart dropped. He pulled out the damp material. Mel's dress.

He staggered back against the wall. Everything about his world was off kilter. Nothing was as it seemed. "It's . . . it's gotta be a lie!" he told himself.

Heading for the front door, he stopped and looked at Alex's body, his face and head almost totally gone. Guilt flooded his system and tears welled in his eyes.

"Alex," he murmured.

Bas blew the horn. Santiago quickly left the house and jumped into his own car, making his escape.

Chapter 14

Chez Rosario

His thick, long dick felt so good inside Melissa's throbbing walls. Bent over, ass up on his water bed, she was biting into the pillow.

"Sing for Daddy," he grunted, pulling her head up by her long blonde ponytail, while he punished her tight, white pussy.

"Ohhhh yessss, you feel so good!" she moaned, having already cum twice and feeling a third explosion on its way. That's why she loved him so much. He knew how to give her multiple orgasms.

"Cum in my mouth. I want to taste you in my throat," she begged.

He pulled out of her pussy, and she quickly turned around. He shoved his dick in her mouth while she three-fingered herself. As he unloaded on her tonsils, she popped herself off to a creamy finish.

He lay back on the bed, and she cuddled up next to him. "I could sleep forever." She giggled, adding, "Thank you, Mr. Rosario."

He chuckled. "Oh, I'm Mister now, huh? A minute ago I was Daddy."

She pecked his lips. "Still are . . . Chez."

He smiled.

Chez Rosario was the eldest of the Rosario Brothers. Next to Santiago, he was the most powerful man in the city. He looked like Big Pun, but just because he was extremely obese didn't mean he was in any way soft. People feared Chez more than Santiago, and Santiago had them petrified.

"So . . . now that we have dispensed with pleasure, what business do you have for me?" he questioned.

She shrugged as she traced his nipple with her pinky nail. "Other than what I told you already, nothing."

Chez laughed. "Baby, how many times have I told you, never tell me anything before we fuck? My mind is on other things," he cracked, caressing her shapely ass.

"Mmmmmmmm, I like that . . . yes . . . well, we now know the bodies in the warehouse belonged to Santiago's most trusted men."

"Is that right?"

Melissa nodded. "And you still say you had nothing to do with it?"

"No, detective, the Rosarios didn't do it," he joked.

She playfully hit him. "So what do you make of it?"

"Interesting." He shrugged.

"I know that look."

"What look?"

She traced his mouth with her finger. "That look . . . you know more than you're letting on," Melissa surmised.

"Doesn't everyone?" he quipped.

"Okay, I know you are not telling me everything, but at least tell me are you and Santiago at war?"

"We've been at war for a long time, but believe me, some wars are fought without firing a single shot," he remarked craftily, as he put two fingers in her wet pussy.

"No mas," she snickered playfully, pulling away.

"I don't know Spanish," he joked as he slid his dick inside her.

After her fifth orgasm, Chez left Melissa feeling sexually fulfilled. Yet her brain was mentally famished for information regarding her case. If Chez Rosario had not bust a single shot at Santiago's dead soldiers, then who did?

Chapter 15

Addicted

Cookie passed Tariq the coke blunt as she drove, head bobbing to the sounds of Rocky ASAP. He inhaled deeply, then again. He was in a zone, a zone he slowly desired to stay in always. Tariq loved the way coke blunts made him feel. He couldn't get enough. Having never been addicted, he didn't know he was flying through signs like a brakeless train.

"We've gotta get some more Goose," Cookie shouted over the music. She turned the bottle upside down to make her point.

Tariq nodded and then made a right, heading to his favorite liquor store. What he saw when he got there, blew his mind . . .

Antonio Rosario.

He was heading in the Chinese restaurant across the street from the liquor store all alone. Tariq couldn't believe his eyes. He did a double take as he drove by, but only caught a glimpse of the back of his head. But his coke-frosted mind assured him it was Antonio.

"Yo, ma, get behind the wheel, all right? I'm about to put in work," Tariq explained as he pulled over.

Being the ride or die bitch she was, Cookie replied, "No doubt."

They quickly exchanged seats as he hit the secret stash in the dash and took the automatic pistol out.

"I got this muhfucka now!" Tariq gritted, rocking in his seat with anticipation. He thought about the reaction Santiago would have about carrying out an unauthorized hit, but the way Tariq saw it, this was an opportunity he just couldn't pass up.

"Double park right here," he told Cookie, pointing to a spot right in front of the restaurant.

She did as told and looked at him. "Do you."

"You already know," he replied as he hopped out.

The restaurant was crowded, and he didn't have anything to cover his face, so he simply pulled his shirt over his mouth and nose.

As soon as he entered, he snuck his intended target from behind. "Fuckin' Rosario rat!" he barked.

"Gun!" somebody hollered.

People quickly scattered, screaming and ducking at the same time.

Bbbrrrrappp!

Tariq let off a blaze of bullets that tore into Antonio's back and head, slamming him up against the counter and spinning him totally around. When Tariq ran up on him to finish the job, he saw that he had made a terrible mistake.

The guy wasn't Antonio.

He didn't even look like Antonio up close. Only upon a fleeting glance had Tariq left the stranger barely clinging to life.

"Oh shit!" Tariq gasped, dropping the shirt inadvertently, revealing his face. Realizing he was exposed, he quickly covered his face. "Don't look at me!"

Brrrrrrrpp! He fired in the air.

"Don't look at me!"

Again, he shot in the air as he made his escape out the door. He leapt in the car, shouting, "Go! Go! Fuck!"

"What's wrong?" Cookie asked, pulling off with tires squealing.

"A muhfucka has his cell phone out! Goddamn, I think he got the license plate!"

As soon as Tariq jumped in the car, he saw the dude as clear as day inside the restaurant holding up his phone videotaping Tariq's escape.

"What you want me to do? Go back?" Cookie proposed, because she was a trooper like that.

"Naw, ain't no time. Fuck!" Tariq cursed, punching the dashboard.

"At least you got the nigguh you was lookin' for, right?"

Tariq looked at her. "Yeah I got somebody . . . the wrong fuckin' man!"

Chapter 16

It's Either You or Me

Asia knocked on Eva's door softly before she entered. She found Eva on the bed, knees up to her chest looking out the window at the full moon.

"Hey. The maid said you were up here," Asia said, sitting on the bed next to her.

"Hey," Eva replied.

She wasn't really in a talkative mood, but Asia was her best friend, and she knew she had come to check on her.

"I heard about what happened at school."

Eva nodded in acknowledgement but didn't speak.

"I think it's fucked up that you got expelled after all the shit Kim's done to you and has gotten away with, you know? And for real, for real, it might be fucked up to say, but she deserved everything you did to her." Asia rubbed Eva's back.

Eva turned her head and looked at Asia. "They said I tried to kill her."

"I know . . . wait, what do you mean *they said*? Did you try to kill her?"

"I don't know." Eva shrugged. "I can't remember."

"Wow, you must've really blacked out on her."

Eva shook her head to fight back the tears. "I'm scared, Asia. Something's happening to me and I can't explain it."

Asia hugged Eva. "Something like what?"

"That's just it, I don't know," Eva answered, wiping the tears with the back of her hand."

"Maybe you were just tired of all the bullshit, you know! Just relax, and in a few days you'll probably remember once your mind is clear."

Eva's face brightened slightly. "You think so?"

"Sure. Now come on. Let's get out of here. You need to breathe, plus you stink."

Eva giggled and hushed Asia playfully.

"Shut up."

"Why don't you go take a shower, and then we can go kick it or something. I've got my mom's Benz," she sang, holding up the car keys.

"Okay, give me a minute."

Eva hopped off the bed and went into the bathroom that was connected to her room. As soon as she heard the shower come on, Asia quickly speed walked down the hall to Tariq's room. The light was off and the door was open. She took one last look up the hallway and then dipped inside.

Asia had to work quickly. She pulled out the bug Detective Mulligan had given her, flipped on the tiny switch, then attached it to the underside of the nightstand. "Sorry, baby, but it's either me or you and the dick ain't that good," Asia quipped, then tiptoed out of the room just as quietly as she had entered.

Chapter 17

Vindication

ike father like son . . .

Those were the words that kept echoing through Santiago's head like a song he couldn't forget.

Like father like son . . .

The phrase came to him in his dreams, mouthed from Alex's dying lips. They came to him when he was awake, as if his mind were whispering them in his own ear.

Like father like son . . .

He sat in the bedroom, gripping a bottle of gin in one hand and a picture of Alex, Bas, and himself in the other. The picture was of their younger days, their invincible days. Each of them staring boldly into the camera, cocky grins on their faces, money in their hands, the world at their feet. They had vowed to live forever, now Santiago's mind was torn between blaming himself and blaming Alex for making him break it. He still didn't know what to believe. All the signs of Mel's infidelity were there. He saw it in her eyes, felt it in his gut. Yet the more rational part of him said he had totally misread the situation. Blinded by a jealous love, he struck out at the wrong person. "Birthday party," he mumbled, scoffing as he hoisted the bottle to his mouth and guzzled.

"You stink."

He heard the words and looked up into Mel's face. He hadn't even heard her come in. The words sounded harsh, but the look on her face wasn't. It reflected concern for her husband. "Look at you. When is the last time you had a bath? Why are you doing this to yourself?"

Santiago looked down at his soiled robe and pajamas. He hadn't been out of the house since Alex's funeral. The only person he communicated with was Bas via cell. He had murdered his cousin, got the devastating news that his son was on the run for murder, and learned a high school counselor called social services on Eva, and they were trying to make his daughter go to a school for troubled teens. Shit was fucked up, and he was beginning to blame his own karma for it.

"It ain't what I'm doin', it's what you did to me," he spat back, swigging from the bottle.

"You're blaming me, Santiago? Really? Wow . . . there was nothing going on between Alex and me, nothing, except in your own jealous mind," Mel spat back.

"Bullshit!" Santiago growled, but he had no conviction behind it, because he wasn't so sure himself.

"No, you know what? It wasn't your jealous mind; it was your guilty mind, Santiago. The guilt in you from all these years of cheating on me with every bitch in the street. You know you deserve the same treatment! But I'm not trying to destroy our marriage, Santiago, you are," Mel huffed.

Santiago shook his head, but deep down, he felt her point. Mel had put up with his bullshit for years, so a part of him felt like it was her turn. But the rest of him wouldn't accept it.

His cell phone rang in his robe pocket. He answered, "Yeah."

"I'm a block away," Bas replied.

"A'ight. I'll be ready in a few."

They hung up. Santiago struggled to his feet. Mel tried to help him up, but he shrugged her off. She glared at him.

"You can't keep pushing me away, Santiago, and expecting me to take it," she warned.

He wanted to reach out to her, but his pride wouldn't allow it. All he could see when he looked at her was her sexy ass fuck faces she probably made while Alex was inside of her.

"Birthday party," he mumbled, then went and took a shower.

When he came out dressed, he saw that Mel was, too. She was standing in the mirror, stepping into her shoes and putting in her earrings.

"Where the fuck you think you goin'?" he questioned, a slight drunken sway in his stance.

She looked at him through the dresser mirror. "Don't start, Santiago."

He took a menacing step toward her. "I asked you a goddamn question."

Tense pause. Conflicting gazes.

"Shopping."

He laughed. "You wanna shop. Go look in that closet and wear the shit you already bought, or better yet, tell that nigguh to buy it. Oh I forgot, he dead!"

Mel shook her head. "You're losing your mind."

"Naw, bitch, you just think I am! I'm still muhfuckin' Santiago, don't ever forget that!" he bellowed.

Mel stared at him with pity. Standing there in his drunken state, he only looked like a shell of his former self.

"Gimme your keys, Mel!" he demanded.

"My what! Oh, *hell no*, nigguh! You goin' too fuckin—"

Slam!

All Mel felt was a vise grip on her throat and the vanity mirror cracking against her back as Santiago pinned her hard against the mirror with fire in his eyes.

133

"Gimme . . . your keys, Mel!" he seethed.

She didn't hesitate to hand him her clutch purse with her car keys in it. He let her go.

"And your phone," he added.

"It's on the bed," she grunted.

"Get it and give it to me," he ordered calmly but firmly.

She stepped around him on wobbly legs, snatched the phone off the bed, then handed it to him, hand on hip, wrist up.

"Happy?" She glared.

"Don't leave this room until I get back, Mel. Do you understand?"

"What if I get hungry?" she quipped with bitter sarcasm.

Santiago glanced around, spotted the bottle of sleeping pills, and tossed them at her. She swatted them away, knowing what he was implying. A not-so-subtle suggestion to eat the whole bottle of sleeping pills, because deep down he wouldn't mind if she did. It wasn't that he didn't love her; he just could no longer trust her because he could no longer trust himself.

"It's a damn shame when a man has to rely on a key to keep a woman," Mel spat with a smirk.

Santiago glared at her as he walked out. He picked out the bedroom key on his key ring, something he had because of the larger safe he kept. Now he had another jewel to lock up. He locked the door and turned just as Eva was entering the hall way.

"Hey Daddy, where's Mommy? I have to talk to her," Eva said.

"Your mother's . . . not feeling well, baby girl. Talk to her later," Santiago replied.

Eva saw the pain in his eyes. "Daddy, are you okay? You know I love you, right?"

Santiago smiled. He loved his baby girl more than anything, so hearing her words cheered him up mentally. She hugged him tight and could smell the liquor coming out of his pores. After the hug, she held him at arm's length and looked into his eyes.

"Daddy, is this about Uncle Alex? Please don't worry, because I know whoever did it will suffer for it soon," she surmised.

He already is, his mind groaned.

"I . . . I know." Santiago gazed at his daughter strangely. "I thought you didn't like violence, baby girl?"

"I don't, but this isn't violence . . . this is vindication," she replied solemnly.

Santiago sensed something different about her, but he was too drunk and distraught to put his finger on it. He kissed her on the forehead and walked away.

*****

". . . and I talked to the mayor, too. He sends his condolences. You know why he couldn't come to the funeral, but he said he'll see you soon. Atlanta is good. Now that them snake ass nigguhs are gone, everybody on their P's and Q's." Bas chuckled, then glanced over at Santiago as he drove. Santiago had his head down, concentrating on Mel's phone as he flipped through it.

"Big Brah, did you hear what I said?"

"Yeah," Santiago lied without looking up, and added under his breath, "This bitch done erased all the texts."

Bas sighed as he stopped at the light. "Big Brah, I know that ain't Mel's phone."

Santiago didn't answer.

"You goin' through her phone now?"

Santiago couldn't even look at him. "Yo . . . I know something is goin' on."

Bas shook his head then pulled off as the light turned green. "For what it's worth, I don't believe that surprise party bullshit either. For real, shit was too deep for a fuckin' party. Alex was makin' real moves. Now whether he knew or was just a pawn, I don't know, but I do know boss when I see it. But bottom line is . . . you can't let that shit fuck with your mind. Real talk, get all the way rid of her, or let her go, but fuck all this sucka for love shit!" Bas huffed.

That was one thing Santiago could always count on. Bas always tells it like it is. He had never been Santiago's yes man, and he respected that. Santiago nodded and took a deep breath.

"I feel you, Lil Brah, but real talk, I love her too much to . . . get rid of her. And I can't let her go. I'm just caught up," Santiago admitted, rubbing his forehead.

They rode in silence for a moment until Santiago finally said, "Yo, make a right. Jump on the highway."

"Where we goin'?" Bas asked as he threw on his blinker.

"Somewhere I should've taken you. I'm takin' you to see Mr. Colon."

Bas looked at him intently, but didn't say a word. There was no need, because he knew exactly who Mr. Colon was. Santiago's connect. The one he inherited from his uncle, Carlos. Santiago had introduced neither Alex nor Bas to the connect over the years, so Bas knew things had to be serious for Santiago to make such a move.

"You sure, Big Brah?"

Santiago chuckled. "Of course I'm sure, yo. I ain't that drunk."

They both laughed.

Santiago continued. "Are you sure you can handle it?"

"Hell yeah I can!" Bas replied with vigor.

Santiago sighed. "And you're right. Where my head is, it's no good for business. I need to get my family together. I'ma take Mel on a nice, long vacation, work shit out. Then when I get back, get Eva back on track. As for Tariq . . ." He shook his head. "I'll think of something."

"Have you spoken to him?"

"Yeah, and I'ma call him in a few. But I want me and you clear first. As of now, you run the family biz, yo. You the only muhfucka I would trust with this type of responsibility, so . . . don't let me down," Santiago warned.

"I won't, Big Brah . . . I won't," Bas replied solemnly.

Santiago nodded, then called Tariq from his mother's phone. The phone rang and rang, leaving him to ponder his every action. He hadn't yet thought of a solid plan to get his son out of the storm of shit he created. That single idea made Santiago ask himself two questions: What the fuck was going on with everybody? Was he responsible for the current condition of his family?

Chapter 18

Mind Blowing

Cookie kissed down Tariq's stomach, planting tantalizing pecks all along the way. As she got closer and closer to his rock hard dick, she angled her body and positioned herself on top of him, her pussy dripping in his face.

Tariq spread her pussy lips and began sucking her clit while Cookie sucked his dick. His phone rang with Santiago's call, but he was too far gone to care. His dick was hard as a rock and Cookie was treating it like rock candy, slurping and groaning like she couldn't get enough. He was devouring her pussy just as greedily, darting his tongue in and out of her wetness while he finger fucked her asshole with two fingers.

"Ohhhh, daddy," she cooed, "you gonna make me squirt!"

Hearing her sexy voice made him finger and suck faster. Cookie couldn't take it anymore; she threw her head back and came all over Tariq's chin and lips.

"Come on, daddy, fuck this pussy good. You got it on fire!" she exclaimed. She turned and planted her feet on the bed as she squatted over Tariq, taking his rock hard thickness in hand and impaling herself on it.

"Ooooooh!" she squealed.

"Yeah, you nasty bitch, take this dick!" he grunted.

And she did, every inch. She put her hands on his chest for balance and began popping the pussy, riding his dick like a pro and filling the hotel room and beyond with her sex song.

Tariq gripped her by her hips and slammed her down on his dick, grinding into her hard and slow. The move took Cookie's breath away. She dug her nails in his chest as the base of his dick rubbed up against her clit, while his head hit her spot.

"Ta-Ta-Ta," she stuttered, unable to get his whole name out of her mouth.

Tariq flipped her over on her back and proceeded to punish the pussy. Cookie grabbed the headboard and took the dick like a big girl.

"Cum for me, daddy. Cum in this pussy," Cookie gasped.

She wrapped her legs around his waist and pulled him closer, using her pussy muscles to squeeze his lustful thrust. The total embrace was too much for Tariq, and he bust long and hard, which triggered another climax in Cookie.

When she finally caught her breath, she wrapped her arms around his neck, kissed him passionately, then said, "See, I told you."

Tariq was still in a daze. He tingled all over. It was the best sex he ever had. But he knew it wasn't just the pussy . . .

It was the crack cocaine . . .

For the first time, he had smoked crack straight. Since they had been on the run, they had been holed up in the motel room, two states away from home. They only went out to get something to eat.

They ran out of weed but not coke.

"Fuck it, it's stronger without weed." Cookie had shrugged.

"You mean smoke it raw? Naw, fuck that. I ain't hittin' no fuckin' pipe!" Tariq said.

"It's not a pipe, yo," Cookie responded as she punched a small hole in the side of a Coca Cola can. She bent the can so the small hole was in the middle of the dent and placed a small chunk of crack on the hole. Tariq had watched as she put the lighter to the rock and inhaled from the mouth of the can. She held the smoke in, then exhaled. And the look on her face was so serene, as if she had just exhaled all of her problems.

She looked at him, eyes glazed with lustful euphoria and spoke the truest words of temptation. "Trust me."

Tariq could smell the burning crack, and it reminded him of the way the blunt smelled, something he already had a jones for.

Cookie seemed to read his mind. "It's just like smokin' it in a blunt, baby. It ain't no different," she reasoned.

"Naw, yo. I ain't no fuckin' fiend," Tariq protested, but this time less fervently.

Cookie sucked her teeth dismissively. "Nigguh, that crack head shit is for weak nigguhs! Nigguhs who can't control they high. You ain't no weak nigguh," she remarked, massaging his ego. She hit the can again. This time, she had his total attention. Seeing that she did, she extended the can to him.

"Here, baby, hit it. I'll suck your dick at the same time. And I promise you . . . it'll blow your mind." Cookie smirked like Eve did to Adam.

Tariq put his lips to the can at the same time Cookie put her lips to his dick. The sensation hit him at both ends and pleasure was indescribable.

Things would never be the same . . .

Chapter 19

The Inevitable End

Santiago stood over the bed watching Mel sleep. She had the face of an angel and the body of a goddess. His eyes traveled her curves, admiring every inch his eyes explored. His breath quickened. He sat down on the side of the bed and gently caressed her cheek. Her eyes fluttered awake.

"Are you hungry?"

She turned away from his caress. "Don't you act like you care now," she retorted.

Mel started to roll away, but Santiago put his hand on her shoulder. "You're right, baby. I deserve that. But don't turn your back on me, okay? I . . . I've been thinkin' . . . we need to go away, just you and me . . . get back to us, you know? Work things out," Santiago suggested.

Mel could see the genuine yearning in his eyes, and for a minute the love she once had for him surfaced. But it was only for the moment because a deeper realization of who he truly was, quickly replaced the emotion.

"I . . . I don't know, Santiago. It's too late for that."

Her words were like a dagger in his heart.

"Don't say that, baby. We can work this out, make things right. We just need some time," he replied, reaching out to pull her to him.

Mel flinched, and in that small gesture, Santiago sensed something he never had to deal with before.

Rejection.

He snatched Mel to him by the arm.

"Santiago, you're hurting me!" Mel yelled.

"I told you don't turn your back on me!"

"Stop it, Santiago! Let me go!"

His heart cried, I can't! But his ego made him reply, "Fuck that! Come here!"

The more she struggled, the angrier he got, until Mel was able to look in his eyes and see that he had truly snapped. That only made her fight harder and elevate the vicious cycle.

Smack!

Santiago pimped-slapped her, then pinned her to the bed by the throat.

"You ain't gave me pussy since that nigguh died! What, your pussy died with him? Fuck that!" Santiago spat.

"Get off of me!" Mel screamed, trying to pry his hand from her throat. He snatched off her bra and her full juicy breasts bounced free. He buried his face in her chest, licking and sucking on her nipples.

"San–Santiago, stop!" she gasped, but for him, there was no turning back.

Her kicking and clawing only pissed him off and turned him on. He ripped off her panties, snatching the flimsy material off her as if it were made of paper.

"Yeah, bitch, this still is my pussy, you understand? My pussy!" he proclaimed, pulling his dick out and plunging inside her tight, moist pussy. Mel tried to squeeze her pussy muscles together, but his powerful thrusts broke right through.

Mel broke down in tears.

"Don't cry now, bitch! This is what you want, ain't it? You dirty bitch! You can fuck him, then you can fuck me!" Santiago bassed.

Imagining Alex fucking Mel made Santiago fuck her harder. Her body went limp as her will gave out and she stopped fighting. He plunged deeper, thrusting faster, imagining the lustful moans she made with Alex, but under him she lay silent.

"Aarrrrgggh!" he grunted hard as he released inside of her, burying his face in her neck.

For several seconds afterward, he lay on top of her trying to gain his composure. When what he had just done finally set in, he was too ashamed to look at her and hated himself for being so weak.

"Are you finished?" she asked coldly.

Silently, he stood up and looked down at her lying there on her back staring at the ceiling. Her facial expression blank. Seeing her lay there, knowing what he just did to her, his manic mood swings swung back to affection.

"Mel . . . I'm sorry. I don't know what came over me. I love you, baby. I . . . I swear, I'm sorry," he stammered, on the verge of tears.

The glare she gave him could've frozen stone.

"You're sorry? Sorry for what, Santiago? Sorry for destroying your family? Sorry for killing your own blood? Wait, let me guess. You're sorry about raping me? Yeah, you're sorry all right. You talk all that shit about being a man, but you ain't shit! You can keep me locked in here and rapin' me 'til hell freezes over, but that won't change the fact that it's over! You hear me? I don't love you anymore, Santiago. Deal with it!"

The poison of her words left him livid and seething. He wanted to break her fucking jaw, but he knew it would only do more harm than good. "Okay, Mel . . . you win," Santiago replied, then walked out leaving her sobbing on the bed.

As he walked away, he heard Bas's voice in his head. *Either get rid of her or let her go . . .*

Now that the inevitable end of his marriage was staring him in the face, he knew he had to reconsider his approach. Mel had been with him a lot of years. She had seen and knew a lot. Could she be trusted to hold water? More importantly, could he afford to take that chance?

As he reached the kitchen, his thoughts were averted by the silhouette of a strange shadow moving across the patio. His street sense kicked in instantly. The elaborate security system he had built in and around the house was set to detect motion and body heat, but since it didn't light up the grounds and send him an alert, he knew it had been somehow bypassed. That told him one thing: whoever it was, was definitely not an amateur.

Santiago kept guns stashed all over the house, so he reached behind the refrigerator for the ten shot Glock 9-millimeter he kept there. As soon as he had it in hand, he let off three shots through the patio window.

Boosh! Boc! Boc!

He saw the first shadow go down, but several other shadows turned and fired simultaneously. Bullets flew everywhere as Santiago dove for cover.

"Who the fuck!" he grumbled, vexed that nigguhs felt comfortable enough to bring it to him in his home.

The thought alone drove him from cover, busting back as he ran for his study. Behind a row of books he had a recessed compartment where he kept fully automatic .380 Smith and Wessons. Shots rang out all around while he clipped the gun up, cocked it back and went to war.

Bap! Bap! Bap! Bap! Bap!

The rapid fire action sprayed bullets like water, dropping two more, but they kept coming like roaches or swarming zombies.

"Daddy, look out!" Eva screamed.

He didn't know she had entered the room, but her presence instantly took all his attention. Instead of looking in the direction of danger, he looked in her direction to make sure she was okay.

"Eva! Get out of—"

Boc! Boc! Boc! Boc!

The first two shots blew him off his feet, the second two spun him around and planted him face down in the carpet.

"Daddy!" Eva screamed.

Her voice sounded garbled in his ears, somehow . . . distant. Santiago wanted to will himself up, but he couldn't move. The pain seared all over, burning and spreading throughout his body like an internal inferno. The pain was unbearable and then . . .

Blackness.

Chapter 20

Dark Future

Santiago woke up handcuffed to a hospital bed. At first he remembered nothing, and all he felt was pain all over. The sunlight coming through the window hurt his eyes.

"He's awake," he heard someone say.

Turning his head, he saw the uniformed officer speak into his walkie talkie. Then it all came back. The shadows, the gunfire, the pain, Eva. "Where's my daughter?" he questioned the officer intently, his voice croaky from non-use.

The officer smirked and walked out.

Several moments later, he re-entered with a nurse and right on her heels was his lawyer, Stephanie Myers.

"How are you, Mr. Acevedo? Here's some water," the nurse offered, pouring him a cup of water and extending it to him.

He ignored the nurse and the water and looked at Stephanie. "Where's Eva?"

Stephanie smiled. "Eva's fine. She—"

"Was she hit?" he asked, preparing for the worse.

"No, not at all. She's downstairs, but they won't let her in."

Santiago breathed a sigh of relief.

"Please drink this, Mr. Acevedo. You'll feel better," the nurse said politely.

He took the water and sipped, then gulped, and before he knew it he had emptied the cup and wanted more. He hadn't even realized he was dehydrated.

"How long have I been here?" he asked.

"Five days," Stephanie replied. "They didn't know if you were going to make it, but I told them you were strong." She winked.

"And why the hell am I cuffed? And why is he here?" Santiago probed, referring to the officer.

"Because you're a fuckin' cop killer, asshole," the officer sneered. The look on his face saying he wished Santiago were dead.

"Cop killer?" Santiago echoed.

"Alleged," Stephanie quickly added, glaring at the officer.

"You mean them muhfuckas were cops? They never identified themselves!"

Stephanie held up her hand. "We'll talk about it later," she told him, using her eyes to refer to the officer's presence.

Santiago sighed hard and wiped his face with his free hand. "When can I see my daughter?"

"When I decide," Detective Melissa Mulligan answered as she came through the door.

As soon as their eyes met, and Santiago saw her arrogant little smirk, he knew he'd hate the bitch.

"Hello, Mr. Acevedo. I'm Detective Mulligan," she remarked, extending her hand for him to shake.

Santiago ice grilled her.

"I didn't think so." Melissa chuckled, taking her hand back. "Anyway, as I was saying . . . pretend I'm a door and your daughter is on the other side of me. Get the picture?"

"Excuse me, detective, but I'm Mr. Acevedo's lawyer, Stephanie Myers."

Melissa looked her up and down with the look two white women reserve for one another in the presence of men. "Yes, figures," Melissa snorted, then turned her attention back to Santiago. "So Santiago, you mind if I call you Santiago?"

"You mind if I call you bitch?" he spat back menacingly.

"*Detective* Bitch, Santiago. I'm sure I don't have to tell you that you fucked up, right? Three officers were shot—one fatally, and you were caught holding the murder weapon. Pretty much open and shut, huh?"

"I have nothing to say," Santiago replied.

"I would think about that if I were you. Believe me, I think you and I could find a lot to talk about if given the chance." She smirked, giving Santiago a playful eye. *I didn't realize he was so good looking up close.*

In her mind she wouldn't have minded giving him some play if she wasn't already in bed with his enemy. Literally.

Santiago turned his head. "Nurse, I need some rest."

"Detective, I think you should go," the nurse responded, giving Melissa a stern look.

"Just one more question, Santiago. Any idea where Tariq is? I'm gonna catch him sooner or later, but if you help me now, I'll make sure you two are cellies on death row."

Pfffff!

Santiago straight spit in Melissa's face. The officer lunged, but Melissa restrained him. Calmly, she used Santiago's bed sheet to wipe her face, then said, "Well . . . we can add assault on an officer to your list of charges. Yes, Santiago, I'm going to have a lot of fun breaking you," Melissa remarked, her mouth smiling but her eyes weren't.

She walked out leaving him to ponder his dark future.

*****

Downstairs, Eva was pacing the floor. She hadn't left the hospital since they had brought Santiago in. All she kept seeing were the criss-crossing infrared beams in their darkened living room. She couldn't get it out of her mind.

Eva had been in her room when she initially heard shots fired. A part of her panicked, but a part of her wouldn't allow her to stay put. She quickly jumped off the bed and ran out the door. When she got downstairs, the first thing she saw was her father and a shadowy figure with an infrared beaming on his back.

"Daddy, look out!"

It seemed every infrared found Santiago and hit his body up from every angle. In that moment, her whole world came crashing down, and one word seared itself in Eva's mind . . .

Vindication.

"Get down on your knees now!"

"Move!"

The shadowy figures barked at her in rapid fire. They trained the guns on her until she was cuffed, and she never took her eyes off Santiago's body.

"Don't worry, Eva, he's gonna be okay," Asia remarked, rubbing Eva's back.

She had been with Eva at the hospital, off and on, all five days, but her motivation was totally different than Eva's.

"I hope so," Eva mumbled, looking down at her folded hands in her lap.

"Have you called Tariq?" Asia questioned.

Eva nodded. "I've tried a million times, but he hasn't picked up."

"You don't have any idea where he might be? He could really be in danger," Asia warned, fishing for more information.

"I wish I did."

Stephanie popped off the elevator and walked over to Eva and Asia. As soon as Eva saw her, she stood up.

"How is he, Miss Myers?" she asked, almost breathlessly.

"He's awake and he's going to be fine," Stephanie beamed.

"Thank God!" Asia exclaimed.

Eva hugged Asia tightly, tears brimming her eyes. "Oh my God! I'm so happy!" Eva remarked.

"Yeah, but he's not out of the woods yet."

Eva turned her head and saw Melissa standing there. She had gotten off the elevator with Stephanie, but Eva hadn't recognized the face. Now, Eva would never forget it.

"Who . . . who are you?" Eva asked.

"Detective Mulligan," Melissa answered, extending her hand to shake, but Eva ignored it. Melissa added, "Yep, you're definitely your father's daughter."

"Detective, Miss Acevedo has not been charged with anything, therefore, if you will excuse us."

Melissa nodded. "By all means, I just wanted to say to Miss Acevedo, that her father and her brother are in a lot of trouble, so if she knows anything and doesn't share it with me, she will be charged," Melissa warned.

Eva glared at her.

I've got to keep an eye on this one, Melissa thought, because the look Eva gave her was so cold, Melissa felt it in her spine.

"Duly noted," Stephanie replied.

"Good," Melissa added, then glanced at Asia and gave her a nod. She acted as if she'd never seen Asia, but dropped her head and looked away. Melissa walked off, taking Eva's eyes with her.

"Don't worry about her, Eva. She's all talk," Stephanie remarked.

But Eva wasn't the one who needed to be worried.

Chapter 21

Greedy

Forty-five miles outside of Brooklyn, Bas pulled up to the small cottage-like home in a cozy suburban neighborhood. The house was so small his big body silver Mercedes seemed out of place parked in front of it. But Mr. Colon kept this particular house because it was low key, just like he liked it. No one suspected that he was one of the biggest cocaine suppliers on the East Coast, and that was because he moved in silence.

Bas knocked on the door and waited for a moment. The door was opened by Mr. Colon's driver and bodyguard, Manuel. He smiled when he saw Bas.

"How are you, my friend?" Manuel greeted, shaking Bas's hand as he came inside.

Bas sighed heavily.

Manuel nodded gravely.

"Yes, we have heard. Come. Mr. Colon is in the garden."

Bas followed Manuel to the backyard. It was filled with rows of tomatoes, peppers, and broccoli. Mr. Colon was in the midst of the garden with a basket picking tomatoes. When he saw Bas he straightened and smiled. Mr. Colon looked like Ricardo Montalban from the TV show *Fantasy Island*, even though he was well into his seventies. He attributed his health to simple living. Bas admired his approach to life.

"I'm so sorry to hear about my old friend," Mr. Colon remarked.

"Yes, but I just got word he just woke up," Bas informed him.

Mr. Colon smiled with relief. "Wonderful!"

"Indeed . . . anyway, I just came out here so that you and I could be on the same page moving forward," Bas said.

Mr. Colon nodded. "Yes, I understand when Santiago brought you out here and told me he was putting you in charge for a while, I totally understood. I've watched the three of you grow up in this game."

"Ever since Carlos." Bas smirked.

Mr. Colon diverted his eyes and stammered, "Yes, yes, may God bless his soul."

"My visit isn't to dredge up the past, Mr. Colon. I'm here to begin a new future."

"I agree."

Bas smiled.

"No, I don't think you do . . . you see, that future doesn't include you. Your services are no longer needed."

Mr. Colon frowned, and before he could say a word, Bas whipped out his silencer equipped .45 and aimed it straight at Mr. Colon's forehead.

Fzzz! Fzzz!

The two muffled shots burst his head open like the tomatoes in his basket. When his body dropped, he fell into the tomato vines face first.

Manuel had been sitting at the small patio table reading the paper. He had been too far away to have heard the conversation, but the two muffled shots instantly got his attention, but it was too late. Even before Mr. Colon's body had hit the ground, Bas had spun and sent three more at Manuel.

Fzzzt! Fzzzt! Fzzzt!

All three shots ripped through the paper and lodged in Manuel's throat, chest, and cheek. He fell backward out of his chair, gasping for air. Bas walked up calmly and stood over him.

"It was . . . you!" Manuel gaggled.

Bas aimed the gun at his head. "Surprised?"

Fzzzt!

Manuel's brain flew out the back of his head and framed his shattered skull like an ink blot. A few drops of blood splattered on Bas's gators. He used the cuff of Manuel's trousers to wipe it clean. He then pulled out his cell phone as he walked around to the front of the house.

"Chez? . . . It's done," Bas reported and then hung up, leaving the two bodies to rot in the afternoon sun.

During the drive, Mr. Colon's words pushed Bas far back into the past, the past when Alex, Santiago, and Bas himself, were on the come up.

"Alex, grab the door! Grab the fuckin' door!" Santiago barked.

He and Bas were struggling with a dude as they tried to drag him up the stairs to the roof.

"Yo man, I'ma have Carlos's money! Come on, yo!" the dude begged, but at the same time giving it all he had.

"Fuck that!" Bas gruffed and kicked the dude in the face, breaking his jaw.

The roof door banged open as Alex had to lay his shoulder into it because it tended to get stuck. They had the dude half way through the door when he grabbed the metal railing along the side and held on for dear life.

"Man, please! It's at my crib!"

"Yo Alex, shoot that nigguh! Shoot him in the hand!" Santiago ordered.

Alex pulled his little .25 from his back pocket, put it to the back of the dude's hand, and blew a hole through it.

"Aarrrgghh!" the dude bellowed, cradling the bloody stump with his other hand.

Santiago stumbled on the dark roof and fell back on his ass. The dude gained his footing and tried to blast by Bas like he was a running back trying to break into the end zone. Bas ended his hopes with a nose-breaking upper cut that dropped him at his feet.

"Pick him up," Santiago told Alex, trying to catch his breath.

Alex and Bas dragged the dude to the middle of the roof and the three men commenced to whooping and stomping dude until he no longer gave any resistance. Santiago squatted down and looked in the dude's face. Even on this dark night, the dude could see the cold evil in Santiago's eyes.

"M–M–Man, I swear, I swear, I got every dime in my safe! Please man, just don't kill me!" dude pleaded fervently.

Santiago chuckled.

"See Paco, that makes it worse. Because if you have the money but didn't give the money, not only did you try to cheat Carlos, you disrespected him as well," Santiago reasoned.

The dude broke down crying like a baby.

"Shh shh, don't cry, sweetheart, don't cry . . . I tell you what I'm gonna do. I'm gonna give you one chance to get the money. One," Santiago offered, holding up one index finger.

Dude stopped crying instantly. "Thank you, man. Thank you!"

"The only catch is, you have to fly home to get it." Santiago laughed.

With that, Bas and Alex both grabbed one arm and one leg, hoisted dude up, then flung him off the roof.

"Noooooo!" dude hollered as they let him go and he soared into open air.

Santiago stood on the ledge of the building, pulled out his gun, and as dude fell, shot his body up. "Take that wit' you on the way down!" Santiago laughed, and Alex and Bas laughed with him.

In those days, Bas idolized Santiago. They had just begun really getting money working for Carlos. And it seemed the gangsta life fit Santiago like a tailor-made Armani with matching gators. He had the looks that drove chicks crazy, the swag nigguhs wanted to emulate, and the heart to do what most feared.

The three young men were making quite a name in the streets, but by far, Santiago's name rang the loudest. At first, that was okay, but the funny thing about idolizing someone is, once you realize you can't be that person, you start to envy them. Envy becomes jealousy and jealousy becomes hate. But in Bas's heart, the hate was still fused with love. That is, until Santiago came to Bas with a proposition he could not turn down.

"Yo, Big Brah, that's crazy! We can't just kill Carlos!" Bas protested.

Santiago was calm, but firm. He had made his decision. Carlos had to go. It wasn't anything Carlos had done. Santiago had simply become greedy. He wanted it all. He wanted to be the boss.

"Why not?" Santiago asked.

"Because he put us on, yo. He our connect! Plus, I mean, goddamn, he's your fuckin' uncle!"

Santiago clasped his hands behind his back as he paced the floor.

"First of all, he put us on, big fuckin' deal. That would've happened anyway. Still, we could've went with Rosario and got on. Secondly, he ain't the connect, he the muhfucka in the way of us gettin' a connect. His connect is a cat name Colon. If something happened to Carlos, Colon would have to fuck wit' us because we'll have all of Carlo's territory," Santiago explained.

For his final point, Santiago paced, but then stepped closer to Bas. Even though Bas was taller than Santiago, the look in Santiago's eyes made him the bigger man.

"And third . . . uncle or no uncle, I'm gonna be the fuckin' boss, and no one . . . no one is gonna stand in the way of that," Santiago said, and with wicked eyes he added, "not even you, nigguh."

Bas got the whole message, even the unspoken part. He knew what Santiago was getting at. Either Bas was with him or against him, and Lord have mercy on anybody who was against Santiago. Along with the subtle hate, love, and envy Bas's heart harbored, the conversation added fear and mistrust. Fear because he knew there was no way he could say no, now that he knew of Santiago's plans. Santiago wouldn't let him walk with that type of information. And the mistrust came from one realization: If he would kill his own blood, he definitely couldn't be trusted.

"I'm with you, Big Brah," Bas said, but secretly his heart concealed a seed that took root and festered, just waiting for the opportunity to bloom.

On a rainy Tuesday, two weeks after Santiago's proposition to Bas, Carlos' funeral was packed. People came from all over to pay their respects. He had his share of enemies, but they were far out-weighed by his friends.

Alex sat in the front row simply staring forward. His father's death had devastated him. Just looking at him, people could see things would never be the same.

When Santiago walked in with Mel on his arm and Bas and his date at Santiago's back, everyone was greeting him like he was the new don. Even Chez Rosario was there to show his respect. Santiago came up to Alex, took his face in his hands, and said, "Today Alex, we are no longer cousins . . . we're brothers."

Alex didn't say anything, because deep down he knew.

After the funeral, when everyone was leaving, Bas hung back telling his lady to go on. He wanted to speak to Alex. His guilt wouldn't let him leave without doing so.

"He will definitely be missed," Bas commented, looking at the flower laden casket.

Alex didn't respond.

"Yo, Alex . . . I know this is tough for you. I lost my pops, too. But yo, just know I'm here. We family for real. Just like Santiago said earlier, y'all ain't cousins, y'all brothers. Well, we're no longer friends, we're brothers, feel me?" Bas said, pouring his heart out.

Still, Alex didn't respond. The silence felt tense, so Bas started to walk away.

"No. Just no longer friends."

Bas turned back. "Huh?"

"I said we ain't brothers, just no longer friends. You think I don't know? Huh? You think I'm so fuckin' slow that I didn't see it coming?"

Bas couldn't do anything but drop his head.

"He even expected it," Alex remarked, nodding at Carlos's casket. "He told me. He said 'Santiago smells like greed.' But I wouldn't listen. Now here we are. And you have the balls to call us brothers!"

"Yo Alex, I don't know what you're talkin—"

"Oh, you know . . . you know. I just want you to know I know! Santiago's my blood, but you . . . one day mi amigo, one day . . ." Alex let his voice drop off as he brushed past Bas.

Feeling trapped between guilt and betrayal, Bas turned to watch him walk away.

Chapter 22

Life

Y ou have to be strong, baby girl," Santiago said firmly, gripping the county jail phone tightly in his hand.

"You have sixty seconds left," the automated operator cut in, adding to the urgency of the moment.

"I'm not that strong," Eva whined, tears streaming down her face, streaking her mascara.

The world is gonna eat her alive, Santiago thought with crushing despair. Hearing the weakness in his daughter's voice made him grit his teeth to hold back the tears.

"You are stronger than you think. You're my blood," he replied, trying to use his tone to impart strength.

"Thirty seconds . . ."

"I love you, Daddy."

"I love you, baby girl."

The disconnection between them felt like the slice of the guillotine, swift and unfeeling. Santiago looked at the receiver in his hands, lost in his own thoughts.

"Yo, you finished?" a gruff, impatient voice spat, bringing him back to reality and his cold surroundings.

Santiago looked up into the jet-black face of a 250-pound gorilla-looking nigguh, built like *The Green Mile* actor, Michael Clarke Duncan. The nigguh grilled him hard. He knew exactly who Santiago was. He was one of those bad type nigguhs who hated from the sidelines. For years he watched Santiago drive by in cars that cost more than his life was worth, and now he felt like the tables had turned and he had the upper hand.

The room got quiet, waiting . . . watching. Santiago knew how he played the situation would dictate how he lived for the unforeseeable future. All of the dudes knew his name and rep. Now in the gladiator school of the county jail, they wanted to see if it should still be respected. Santiago extended the receiver to the dude, wearing a smile. As soon as he reached out to take it, Santiago fully extended it, bashing him in the mouth with the phone. Blood sprayed from his lips and Santiago went to work. He punched dude in the Adam's apple and that made him gasp for air. Then Santiago brought his face down straight into his knee.

"Oomph!" the big dude bellowed; his bell rang from the blow.

As soon as he hit the floor, Santiago was on him, gripping him by the ears and ramming his head over and over on the concrete floor. By the third blow, dude was out cold, but Santiago kept banging his head, working on permanent brain damage or worse.

"Move! Move! Now!" an officer barked, as several of them rushed in to break up the beating.

They tackled Santiago to the floor, pinning his arms behind his back, mace cans aimed already, in case he gave the slightest resistance.

"Take this animal to lock up and get medical here ASAP!" the female sergeant ordered.

They scooped Santiago up and frog marched him out the door.

"Well, Mr. Acevedo, I see you didn't take long to make your presence known. Now it's my turn to let you know who runs this place," the sergeant bassed.

Santiago didn't even bother to look in her direction. All he wanted to do is get to the cell to be alone with his thoughts. They took him to a tiny, almost closet like cell. A sliver of a window, a slab of steel for a bunk, a sink and a toilet in the corner. They slammed the door behind him, then opened a slot in his door where his food would be pushed through.

"Stick your hands out, Acevedo," the sergeant told him.

He did. She took the cuffs off, then slammed and locked the slot.

"We'll bring you a mat when we get around to it."

Santiago finally looked at her, with the intent of cursing her out for all of her taunts, but what he found wasn't a gruff sergeant bull dagger, but an Angela Bassett looking older woman with a twinkle in her eye that said everything he needed to know.

"Whateva," he replied, deciding to play along and be just as gruff.

A slight grin creased her lips as she turned and walked away.

Santiago sat on his bed and grabbed his head in his hands. After living a life of luxury, shot calling, and doing it his way, was this the way it ended?

Life . . .

The word rattled around in his mind like an annoying screw loosened from its purpose. Every time he heard the word, it seemed to be punctuated with the slamming of a steel door.

"Fuck that!" he growled, standing up to pace the cell.

Outside, the sun was just beginning to disappear, sending oblong shadows stretching across his cell and shading his face in grimy shadows. He stopped in front of the dingy mirror. His usually clean face needed a shave badly.

Life.

He knew what he was facing, but he also knew he could beat it. All he needed to do was to get word to his trusted right hand man, Bas.

"I gotta talk to him," Santiago said to himself.

He just didn't know that Bas wasn't where his problems ended . . . it was where they began.

Chapter 23

Two Selves

I don't trust anyone."

"Puedes confiar en mí."

"Why should I trust you?"

"Soy justo como usted."

"You're just like me. That's deep."

The conversation echoed in Eva's mind in English and Spanish simultaneously, as if she had two minds, two consciences . . . two selves. She lay across the bed blowing the blunt smoke up in the air, her thoughts mangled, tangled, confused but clear.

"Eva."

Losing Santiago was a blow to her world. All her life, Santiago had been there to take care of her, protect her. Now with him gone, she didn't have anyone to help her.

Eva. I'm here and I'll never leave you. I'll take care of you."

"But who are you?" she asked, uncertain if she was addressing an actual voice or a thought.

"Eva! Bitch, I know you hear me!" Mel barked.

Eva sat up, startled, heart banging a hundred miles a rip. She wanted to hide the blunt, but it was too late.

"Goddamn, you just feelin' yourself, huh?" Mel smirked, referring to the blunt.

Eva started to dud it in the ashtray.

"I–I didn't know . . ."

"Don't put it out, pass it." Mel giggled, sitting on the edge of the bed and accepting the blunt from Eva. She looked at it. "This better be some good shit."

Her comment loosened Eva up a little and she laughed. "That's all I smoke."

"I know that's right," Mel replied, taking a small chirp of a toke, then two more, the third making her snort and cough. "Goddamn, what is that? Rocket fuel?"

"Sour diesel," Eva answered, hitting it like she had it mastered.

"Listen, baby, I know you're probably missing your father. I understand that. But I want you to know everything's gonna be okay. It's gonna hurt, but we will survive," Mel said, holding Eva's hand.

It wasn't often that Mel was gentle with Eva, so the gesture didn't go unnoticed.

"I–I . . . I never told you this, but . . . your grandfather, my father . . . I watched him and my mother get killed right in front of my eyes," Mel said, shutting her eyes tight against the pain.

"Oh my . . . God!" Eva whispered, having had no idea.

Mel nodded. "That's why I'm so hard on you, Eva. Because I know how devastating things can be when we lose our safety net. And I want you to know how to be strong," Mel explained.

"I–I understand, Mama," Eva answered, sniffing away the tears.

Mel gently took the blunt from her hand and hit it once more before duding it in the ashtray. She blew out the smoke and said, "Because you're gonna have to grow up quick, Eva. So just now, not only are you a woman, but you're a bad bitch, and a bad bitch not only survives, she lives."

Eva nodded, taking it all in.

Mel continued, the weed making her tongue loose. "Because me? Yeah, I had to go through a lot, but look at me now. Look at us. If I wasn't a bad bitch, I could just as easily be in the projects, broke and fucked up. Now don't get it twisted, it ain't just your looks that make you a bad bitch. It's plenty of pretty bitches stripping for nickels, waiting on the first and fifteenth. You got to know how to work what you got and not let it work you," Mel said, schooling Eva.

"I feel you, Ma." Eva laughed.

Mel ran her hand through Eva's long, silky black hair, a tinge of jealousy in her heart. "Looks can be a double-edge sword, Eva. Remember that." With that, Mel stood up and headed for the door, then stopped and added, "and also . . . remember, a man can always be replaced, because a nigguh need a bad bitch, but a bad bitch don't need a nigguh because any nigguh will do." Mel snickered and walked out.

Eva agreed with everything she said, except about any man being replaceable. In her heart, no man could replace her father, and she was prepared to ride for him to prove it.

Chapter 24

A Matter of Time

If smoking crack is a car on a road to destruction, then Tariq was smoking one hundred miles an hour, going downhill with no brakes. His trip to the bottom had been so quick, because he had something most crack heads didn't have.

Money.

He wasn't able to see that he was addicted because he always had it in abundance. When he went on the run, he took one hundred thousand dollars with him, and at the rate he was going, he was trying to burn every dollar of it up in smoke.

"Shhhh!" He shushed Cookie. "You hear that?"

She waved him off and reloaded the pipe.

"Nigguh, you trippin'."

"Trippin' my ass. I know I heard walkie talkies," he swore, going over to the door and peeping out the blinds.

He had to hold his pants up with one hand because he had lost ten pounds being holed up in the hotel room, smoking, fucking, and barely eating.

Fffffffff!

Cookie's pipe sizzled, sounding like frying bacon. After she exhaled, she snorted, "Riq, 'er time you get high you hear the police or somethin'! Come on and hit this before I smoke it all," she warned.

He knew she was right. The rocks had him bugging. He had even broken up his phone because every time it rang, he'd think it was the police. He'd see the caller ID and exclaim, "The police got Eva! The police got Bas! The police got Santiago!"

No matter who called, in Tariq's cracked out, paranoid mind, the police had gotten them and were calling to set him up. He even thought they could listen to him when the phone was off. So he smashed his and only used Cookie's.

But this time, he wasn't hearing things.

The hotel manager had begun to get suspicious. The couple rarely left the room except late at night, and any time he tiptoed by their door, a strange smell wafted from under it. He thought they were using the room as a meth lab, and he was afraid they'd blow up the hotel. So he got the license plate from Tariq's car and reported it to the police. Once they ran it, and Tariq's name came back, they knew they had a fugitive.

Tariq went back to the bed, and as soon as he put the pipe to his lips, they heard a knock on the door. The pipe went one way and Tariq went the other.

"It's the police!" he grumbled hoarsely, snatching his gun from under the pillow.

Seeing the coke fly out of the pipe, Cookie was on her hands and knees looking for the crumbs.

"Nigguh, is you crazy? You spilled the shit!"

"Fuck that! It's the fuckin' police!" he raved.

They knocked again.

"Hello? Anyone in there? It's the manager," called the voice from the other side.

Cookie breathed a sigh of relief, then sassed Tariq, saying, "Nigguh, it ain't the goddamn police. It's the manager."

"Don't open the door," he warned, gun in hand.

She waved him off dismissively, then opened the door. "Hel—" was all she got out, before the door was forced open, and a sea of police rushed inside.

"He's got a gun!"

"Gun!"

"Don't move!"

"Get down on the ground now!"

A cascade of conflicting commands froze Tariq in his place. He quickly dropped the gun. He was bum-rushed by several officers so hard, that when they slammed him against the wall, the sheetrock cracked.

"Goddamn, that's my arm!" Tariq screamed in agony.

"Stop resisting!"

"I'm not resisting!"

Within seconds, both he and Cookie had been subdued, cuffed, and were being led to separate cars.

"Stupid bitch! I told you it was the fuckin' police!" Tariq seethed.

"I'm sorry, baby. I'm sorry. I didn't know," she sobbed as the officer palmed the top of her head and forced her into the backseat of the squad car.

"You have the right to remain silent . . ."

*****

They kept Tariq in a small filthy holding cell for over six hours with an old drunk who couldn't hold his gas. Tariq paced most of the time while the old man passed gas.

"Ay yo! If you do that shit one more fuckin' time, I'ma beat your old ass!" Tariq threatened, unable to bear the smell anymore.

"Hiccup! Better out than in," the old geezer wheezed.

Tariq shook his head, and kept pacing as an officer walked by.

"Ay yo, officer! Officer! Yo, when I'ma be booked? I been back in this bitch all night," Tariq complained.

"Then what's the rush?" the officer snidely replied, never breaking stride.

"Fuckin' bitch-ass white boy!" Tariq yelled after him.

Brrrrrrrrrtttttt!

The old man let out a monstrous explosion and Tariq lost it. He ran up on the old man and kicked him in the ass repeatedly.

"Nasty! Disrespectful motherfucka!" Tariq barked, kicking him to punctuate every word.

"Uh-oh!" the old man grunted, holding his ass. "Now I done shitted."

Tariq wanted to kick him again, but he was scared he'd get shit on his shoes.

"Ay yo, somebody better come get me before I kill this old motherfucka!" Tariq bellowed through the bars.

"Don't you think you are in enough trouble, Tariq?" Melissa quipped as she rounded the corner and approached the holding cell.

Tariq mean mugged her. "Who you?"

"Proper English and complete sentences, Tariq. Don't be a stereotype," she replied with a smirk, flashing her badge.

"You ain't B-more PD," Tariq remarked.

"Now I've come to take you home. That is, unless you're enjoying yourself in charm city. Officer, cuff him up and escort him to interrogation, please," Melissa requested.

The officer did as she asked. When they got in the room, the officer sat Tariq on one side of the desk, while Melissa propped up on the corner of it. The officer walked out.

"You on a diet or something, Tariq?" she remarked.

"I got nothin' to say, so you wastin' your fuckin' time," he replied.

"Good, because I brought you in here to listen. I would say you fucked up, but that would be cliché, huh? Yeah . . . but I will say, it doesn't have to be this way. I mean, after all you've said, you're probably in more trouble with Santiago than you are with the law," Melissa snickered.

Tariq sucked his teeth, avoiding eye contact. Melissa slid off the table and came around to him. She leaned in close to his ear.

"What do you think papi would say about his son being a crack head? Remember Santiago's rule against dealing with addicts," she said.

But she didn't need to remind him. The thought had colored his every sober moment in the hotel and sent him running back to the solace of the high. He knew Santiago's hatred for people who couldn't control their high. He had seen Santiago beat several men to death simply for stealing from him to get high. Tariq took comfort in the fact that he was his son, but a small part of him knew even that wouldn't be enough to save him.

The look on Tariq's face said it. Melissa smiled.

"Are you wondering how I know about Santiago's rule, or your breaking it? Probably both, huh? Let's just say a little birdie told me."

"You mean a little stool pigeon." He gritted.

She shrugged, propping up on the desk right beside him.

"Tomato tomato, the bottom line is your days may be numbered, and I am the only one who can save you," she offered.

Tariq laughed in her face. "Bitch, please! Yo, bust the door 'cause this conversation's over!"

"Suit yourself, Tariq. Just remember what I said when you're in that cell feenin' for one blast, just one while at the same time worrying when your daddy's gonna come in there and shank you," she taunted.

He looked at her, confused.

"Oh, you don't know? You didn't know Santiago is locked up? What a newsbreak! Turns out his cousin Alex must've been getting high too because Santiago murdered him with his own hands."

The news took Tariq off guard. "You lyin' bitch!" he growled.

Melissa snickered. "True, but not this time. Anyway, you'll see soon enough. He's waiting for you back in the county jail. Boy, is he pissed at you . . . like I said, remember my offer." She winked.

"Go to hell!" Tariq spat, but without the force of conviction.

He'll break, Melissa thought, fully amused. *It's just a matter of time.*

Chapter 25

Betrayed

Bas sat in the armchair that fronted the room. Several of Santiago's top street lieutenants stood around. They looked to him for direction. He was getting used to the feeling of power and he liked it.

"Now that Santiago is gone, we're gonna have to make a few changes," Bas began.

"What kind of changes?" one lieutenant asked.

"Whatever I say we change!" Bas spat, because he was feeling himself.

His look seemed to dare anyone to challenge him, but no one picked up the gauntlet. Satisfied, he sat back.

"Now basically, I feel like Santiago ain't been lettin' y'all nigguhs eat like y'all should. I ain't no greedy muhfucka, so I'll unball that tight fist, all right?"

The lieutenants nodded and murmured their approval, just like Bas knew they would.

Greedy motherfuckas, he thought.

"But in order to do that, we're gonna need a new connect. So . . ." Bas said, as he stood up, 'I want y'all to meet our new connect."

Chez Rosario walked from the back of the apartment and stood beside Bas. Bas put his arm around his neck.

"I can tell by the look on your faces you know exactly who this is, but what I want to know is who the fuck has a problem with it?" Bas looked around the room for signs of disagreement.

"Shit, as long as we eatin', I'm wit' whatever," one of them replied.

Bas chuckled. "My kind of nigguh," he remarked, but inside he was shaking his head. Lack of loyalty was contagious.

"Then that's what it is then," Bas concluded, "except . . . one more thing."

The two gunmen in the back had been waiting on the cue. Once Bas gave it, they rushed out, Mac 11s locked and loaded, and let loose on the unsuspecting lieutenants. No one had a chance to react. The bullets ripped through them like bolts of electricity, twisting and turning their bodies to the rhythm of the gun. When the deafening rapid fire barrage echoed into silence, the lieutenants lay strewn about in bloody heaps. Bas surveyed the carnage.

"They were ready to roll. Why'd you give the signal?" Chez asked curiously.

Bas shrugged. "Shit . . . if Santiago couldn't trust them, how could I?"

Once Bas ensured that most of his ducks were in a row, he headed to Santiago's home to pluck the next to the last duck.

"They've got Tariq," Bas announced as he sat on the couch next to Eva. For a moment she wondered where he came from. It was too close to midnight, and she had just come downstairs to watch *Columbiana* on the 75-inch plasma. She was wearing an oversized Patriot's football jersey, so she felt a little uncomfortable, but it quickly passed as she focused on what he said.

"Where?"

"Baltimore," Bas replied.

Eva sat there trying to let everything sink in. First Alex, then her father, and now Tariq. It's like everyone she loved was being systematically eliminated. She couldn't hold back the tears.

"Why is this happening?" she sobbed, her face buried in her hands.

Bas put his arm around her and hugged her close. "Don't worry, Eva. I've got you now. I'll take care of you," he said in a comforting tone.

She nodded and then kissed him on the cheek. "Thank you, Uncle Bas."

Her lips felt warm, wet, and soft on his cheek. Her young, tender body, heavenly against his. His hand wandered from her shoulder to her hip. The caress sent off warning signals in Eva's head.

"Uncle Bas, what are you doing?" she protested, trying to pull away, but his large arm held her in place.

"I told you . . . I'ma take care of you," he replied, revealing the real intent of his earlier words.

"No . . . don't!" Eva squirmed.

Her protests were nothing in the face of his passion. He had been fantasizing of this moment for too long. Watching her young mare-like body blossom into a stallion. He pulled her onto his lap, pinning her arms at her side.

"I'm your daddy now," he leered, sliding his big beefy hand under her jersey. He ran his hand over her panties, feeling her plump pussy through the fabric.

"Mmmmmm, this pussy is fat," he groaned with pleasure, lying her down on the couch.

"Please, Bas. Please!" she begged, fighting with all she had.

"That's what I aim to do," he growled, snatching her jersey up and revealing her shapely body.

Seeing her full firm breasts and wide, sexy hips drove Bas crazy. He snatched her panties down and dropped his pants around his ankles. Eva caught a glimpse of the biggest dick she'd ever seen in her life. Bas grabbed her by the ankles and spread her legs, positioning his long, extra thick dick to go up in her with one powerful thrust.

"Mommy! Oh God! Mommy!" she cried out, hoping like hell her mother heard her.

Bas invaded her, filling her up and taking her breath away. He had to fight to overcome his urge to not come right then and there. He bit down hard on his bottom lip, still gripping her ankles firmly.

"No pleasssssse stoppp!" she pleaded, until the voice inside of her silenced her in rapid fire Spanish. *Shut up! Shut up! Don't you dare cry out. Don't you make another fuckin' sound! Don't give him the satisfaction!*

Eva went deathly silent. Bas thought she had passed out as women were known to do from the power of his dick, but when he looked, her eyes were closed and her face, expressionless.

"Oh, you a big girl, huh? You wanna show daddy you can take all this dick, huh?" He cocked her legs back, folding her almost and proceeded to punish her with steady pounding thrusts.

Her whimpers caught and died in her throat. Even when her body betrayed her and she came back to back, she didn't make a sound.

"Yeah, baby, this dick good, ain't it? You may not say it, but you feel it!" Bas cackled.

At that moment, Mel came and stood in the doorway. She had just gotten out of the shower after Bas dicked her down. She stood poised and relaxed.

"That's right, daddy. Teach the bitch what life is all about." Mel snickered.

Hearing her mother's voice, Eva's eyes popped open. Mother and daughter's eyes met. Then just as abruptly as she had appeared, she turned and walked away. Eva's eyes followed her into the shadows, but it wasn't Eva who was looking at her.

Chapter 26

Karma

The banging of keys against the steel cell door woke Santiago from his sleep. He rolled over and angrily peered over his shoulder.

"What?"

"Cuff up," the female sergeant ordered him.

He squinted in the dark at his watch that read 3:48 a.m. He sat up but didn't get up. "For what?"

"Because I said so," she shot back like a drill instructor.

Not wanting to give them any reason to keep him in the hole, he threw back the cover, slid his feet into his shower shoes, and then went to the door, wearing only his county issued boxers. Santiago stuck his hands out the trap.

"Behind your back. Cell search," she told him.

"At four in the fuckin' morning?" he bassed, voice still croaky with sleep. He sighed and put his back to the door, then slid his hands out. "This some bullshit yo," he mumbled.

She opened the door, then looked him up and down. "Step away from the door."

Santiago stepped back to the middle of the cell. He should've known something was up when she didn't radio for the lights in his cell to be turned on, and she came in alone, whereas two officers are required for a cell search. She shut the door behind her without letting it lock, then approached him wearing a curious expression. Up close like that she looked even more like Angela Bassett.

She walked around him in a tight circle, looking him up and down.

"Hmph, you ain't so tough . . . shot caller, big balla. Your ass fit in a cell too, I see." She chuckled.

"Ay yo, do your job. I'm tired."

She stopped in his face. "Nigguh, you ain't runnin' shit here . . . I am," she sassed him, then she saw the recognition register in his eyes. "Oh, I see, you remember me, huh? Yeah . . . you remember."

"Mercedes," he replied, keeping his expression neutral.

The dime-piece had been a stripper in one of his clubs a few years back, one that had caught his eye. She was caramel brown with a body that could make a nigguh lock eyes if you tried to follow every curve. Even though her police uniform was loose fitting, there was no denying there was a stallion underneath.

He fully expected her to be on some bullshit, because after only a few weeks of hard dick, he got bored, cut her off cold turkey, and hadn't looked back since.

Karma is a motherfucka.

"That's all you got to say? Mercedes. After how you dropped me like that, I'd figure you'd have plenty to say," she retorted, neck on roll. If she expected Santiago to cop a plea because she had the upper hand, she had him fucked up.

"Bitch, ain't shit changed. I wouldn't give a fuck if you had on a black robe in the courthouse, or the throw-switch to the goddamn electric chair I was sitting in. You should be grateful I remember your sexy ass because a sexy bitch comes a dime a dozen. Now, do what you came to do and get the fuck out of my face," he spat coldly.

Mercedes just shook her head. "Santiago Acevedo . . . the only nigguh I know that can make a compliment sound like an insult. I see you still think it's all about you."

"It is."

"Hear you tell it. Mphh! You lucky you so fine and this dick so good 'cause I could make your life in here a living hell. But since it's you"—She purred, pulling his dick out of the boxer's slit and pumping it to life—"I'ma make it a living heaven." She kissed along his neck to his lips while she stroked his dick.

"Goddamn, ma, you ain't have to go through all that to get this dick." He chuckled, kissing her back.

"I had to make you sweat for the way you did me," she pouted, dropping her police belt to the floor, then unbuckling her pants.

"Yeah, but I don't sweat, I just steam. Now take these cuffs off a nigguh, so I can get right," he urged.

"Next time." She winked as she dropped low and got her eagle on. When she took his dick in her mouth, it felt so good it curled his toes and his shower shoes. Her full, pretty lips had him fucking her face, wishing he could grab her by the arms at the same time.

"Goddamn, ma, you gonna make a nigguh bust!" he grunted.

"Not before I get mine you ain't," she said, after popping him out of her mouth with a slurp. She pushed him back, causing him to bump his head on the wall when he flopped down.

"A'ight now," he warned.

Mercedes stepped out of one of her pants legs.

"Shut up and take it out on this pussy," she said, turning to ride him reverse cow girl style.

She gripped his dick and sat down, taking it all at once and letting out a sexy ass sigh as she leaned forward and grabbed her ankles. Santiago started punishing the pussy from the jump.

"Yeah, daddy, just like that! Beat this pussy good!" Mercedes squealed.

"You love this dick, don't you, bitch?" Santiago gritted, biting his bottom lip while he bounced her hard on his dick.

"Yes, yes!" She shivered, feeling so good she wanted to cry. She leaned back, her back against his chest, cocked her legs up, and began grinding hard. Santiago grinded back just as forceful. She was moaning so loud, Santiago was afraid somebody would hear them.

"Shut the fuck up before you get us busted!" he warned.

"I-ooh–I can't help iiiiitt!" she squealed, her pussy erupting with a creamy explosion.

As soon as she came, she hopped up and put on her pants. Santiago's dick was standing straight up.

"Thanks," she replied, buckling her police belt.

"Hold up. I ain't get me," Santiago protested, dick so hard it was quivering.

"Next time." She winked with a giggle.

"Oh, word up? It's like that?"

"Give you something to think about. Bet you won't forget my sexy ass now!"

Santiago couldn't help but laugh. Mercedes wouldn't forget him as well, and he knew he would put her to good use. His conscience entered and left him with a thought that would keep him awake for most of the night. Perhaps his current dwelling place did mean karma had come to repay, and Mercedes was a mere reminder, a small fraction of his mistreatment of women.

Nevertheless, Santiago had business to accomplish and would play her thoroughly until each of her strings snapped.

Chapter 27

Invisible Leash

(Basim and Mel's Story)

He had seen her first . . .
That night in the Chinese restaurant, while Mel was sitting there thinking her life was ending, only to find out it was just beginning.

When Bas had walked in, the chime of the bell over the door alerted her to his presence. For five glorious seconds, Mel was all his. She was the most beautiful woman he had ever seen. Her radiant skin seemed to glow in his eyes.

Mel could tell by the look in his eyes that she could wrap him around her finger. For Bas she was Mrs. Right. But for Mel, he was Mr. Right Now.

Until Santiago walked in five seconds later.

The way she blew Bas's mind, Santiago blew hers. She instantly believed in love at first sight because she just knew she was in love. Her heart bapped, her pussy creamed, and his smile made her want to suck his dick on the spot.

"Lookin' for me?" Santiago quipped knowingly, seeing the lust in her eyes.

Mel had a slick mouth from all the years on the street, but Santiago made her feel like a little bitty girl.

"Yes," she replied.

He sat down at her booth. "What's your name, sweetness?"

"Melanie . . . Melanie Verley."

"No it's not," he smiled mischievously.

"Huh?"

"It's Melanie Acevedo and I'm Mr. Acevedo," Santiago charmed and she was a wrap from there.

Bas was crushed and heated at the same time. He had seen her first, but it was clear whom she had chosen. Still, deep down he yearned for her.

He just knew he'd get his chance because Santiago got bored with women quickly and discarded them like outfits that once fit but were now just old clothes. But not Melanie. She was different.

"Let me find out, nigguh." Bas chuckled like he was joking, but he was really signifying.

"Find out what?" Santiago replied.

They were driving along in Santiago's second Rolls Royce.

"That you 'bout to burn the black book for Lil' Mama. You act like y'all attached at the hip!"

Santiago laughed liked a man in love. "Chill yo. Never that. But I can't lie. I'm feelin' for her though."

Bas's heart dropped. "Yeah yo, that's what's up . . . I'm happy for you," he lied.

"Besides, I wouldn't burn the black book," Santiago joked. "I'd give it to you!"

Bas took the joke like a slap in the face, but he showed his teeth to hide it.

As for Mel, her street instincts told her Bas could be useful. She knew how he felt about her because she could see it in his eyes every time he looked at her. She didn't encourage it, but like the bad bitch she was, she kept him on an invisible leash that her slightest gesture could pull.

"I like your lady friend, Bas. She's pretty. She reminds me of someone," she remarked in passing one night at the club.

If Bas would've had a tail, he would've wagged.

Over the years, she used Bas to keep her informed on Santiago's side chicks and affairs. He used this to his advantage as well, because he learned to manipulate her through the fact that she hated light-skinned bitches with long hair.

"Yeah, she a'ight, but just another red bone, you know how Santiago do," Bas remarked off handedly, even though the girl he was talking about was cinnamon brown.

Mel turned red under her chocolate skin, sucking her teeth and blowing the comment off. "Whateva! I don't give a fuck about Santiago's whores, 'cause that's all they are. Ain't nann bitch livin' in no mansion, diamonds on flash like this bitch," Mel huffed.

"Yo, why you put up with it anyway?" Bas questioned.

Because I love him, her heart answered, but her pride made her reply, "Because he takes care of home."

"Yo ma, any man would do that for you. Nigguhs will break their backs for you just to keep a smile on your face, or turn your tears into diamonds. All that beautiful chocolate, who would settle for vanilla?" Bas smirked, playing to her vanity.

Mel cracked a sly smile. "So what are you trying to say, Bas? That I should leave Santiago for . . . any nigguh?" she probed, playing with his emotions.

His eyes said 'you know what I'm saying,' but his fear of crossing the line with the boss's wife made him reply, "I'm just sayin', ma, you a jewel . . . and any nigguh that has you should treat you like one."

Their cat and mouse game went on until a chain of events set off the plan that would ultimately destroy them all.

On a day when all seemed well, Bas spoke words that figuratively ripped Mel's womb wide open.

"He what!" Mel spazzed, grabbing her stomach and stumbling back from the sting of the words she heard.

Bas was taken aback by the force of her reaction. She had never flipped like that before, but then again, he had never told her one of Santiago's whores was pregnant and Santiago had gotten her a condo.

"I'm sorry to tell you that Mel, but it's true." Bas smiled.

Those were the words that jumped in Mel's mind. *Santiago must be planning to replace me.* Mel could see how his womanizing had gotten to be blatantly disrespectful. Ever since the incident on the boat, he had gotten bolder and bolder with his bullshit. He had even started fucking their housekeeper and forbade Mel to fire the bitch!

She took it all as a sign that it was something she wasn't doing. She blamed herself and bent over backward to anticipate and accommodate his needs. This only made Santiago push the envelope.

"What would you say to a threesome?" Santiago had asked her one day. His eyes dared her to say no, but truth be told, Mel welcomed the chance. Miss Brooks had left a permanent sweet tooth in her mouth for the taste of a woman and she thought, If he was going to cheat, was it really cheating if she was a part of it?

Watching her man giving another woman pleasure in their bed, a light-skinned bitch at that, made Mel sick to her stomach. She went through the motions, but when they finished, she told Santiago, "Don't ever ask me to do it again."

He just smiled and walked away.

Now Bas was telling her what amounted to the straw that broke the camel's back.

"What's her name?" Mel wanted to know.

"Monet," he answered.

She almost threw up. That was the same bitch they had a threesome with! He made Mel lick that bitch's pussy! Mel was so enraged she was dizzy. She staggered a step, but Bas caught her in his powerful arms.

"Ma, you okay?"

The overwhelming nature of the moment, the open wound of her emotions, and genuine sincerity in his tone was too much for Mel, and she broke down in his arms. "How could he do this to me? How?" Mel sobbed, truly devastated by the situation.

Even though she was heartbroken, her survival instincts were never far from the surface. Above all else, Mel was a survivor, and her cunning mind began to weave a web of deception.

She turned her face to his and kissed him softly, almost as if it were a mistake. A soft brushing like the strike of a match that ignited a passion already aflame in Bas's soul. He devoured her kiss, embracing her tightly in his arms. She could feel him against her stomach, growing and growing and growing and . . .

His length and size scared and attracted her at the same time, and even though knowing all that dick was only inches away made her pussy purr, she knew if she gave him her sex, the greater power she had over him would be gone. Reluctantly, but with calculated hesitance, she pulled back.

"I–I–I–can't. I–I don't know. I'm confused," she sobbed, but this time her tears were crocodile.

"Baby, I'm here, and I promise I ain't goin' nowhere. I know you know how I feel for you, Mel. I love you, ma!" he pledged.

Mel pulled out of his embrace. "I know, Bas, and truthfully, I have feelings for you, too . . . but we can never be. Santiago would never let me go. I think he gets off on keeping me a slave. And even if he did, he'd never see you with me. He'd think you had been checkin' for me, and then he wouldn't trust you. And you know what happens to people he doesn't trust," she reminded him.

Bas paced the floor in short bursts. He had, had a taste of Mel, and now there was no turning back. He had to have her. But a part of him feared Santiago.

Mel walked up to him, pinned him with her gaze, and asked, "Who is your loyalty to? Me or . . . him?"

Bas paused long enough to fully digest her question, but quick enough to signal total devotion when he took her hand and put it on his heart, so she could see how fast it was beating.

"Who do you think?" he replied.

She smiled, then kissed him briefly but passionately. "Then love will make a way," she assured him.

But love didn't find a way . . . she did.

Mel knew Santiago's weakness was an innate superstition. She knew he still felt guilty about killing Carlos, so Santiago felt like, sooner or later, karma would catch up with him.

"Baby," Mel began one night while massaging his shoulders (but she really wanted to wring his neck), "you had a good run. When are you gonna let the life go?"

"Let it go?" He snorted. "For what?"

"Think about it, daddy. You know better than anybody how far you've come and what you had to do to get here. But, it's a reason for everything and a time for things to come back around," she warned.

He snorted again, but he didn't say anything. She knew he was listening. "Besides, Alex . . . he's been loyal to you despite . . . everything. He'd love to be the boss, and deep down, you know he deserves it. That way you can play the background, but still pull the strings."

Santiago had been thinking along the same lines somewhat, so her words made sense. Besides, this wasn't the first time Mel had given him words of wisdom on the game. He knew she knew the game as well.

"Yeah yo . . . I hear you," he replied in a non-committed tone.

She kept the idea in her head, subtly, like only a woman can, and while she worked him, she worked Bas at the same time. It was obvious that Alex and Bas weren't seeing eye-to-eye. They were a team, but at the end of the day they went their separate ways.

"Santiago is planning on retiring," she told Bas one day, then casually added, "and I think he's gonna put Alex in charge."

That comment instantly got Bas's attention. He knew if Alex became boss, it was over for him. But at the same time, he felt Santiago was setting him up. With Santiago retiring, what better way to ensure Bas's silence than with his death? And knowing the bad blood between Alex and Bas, why not let Alex do his dirty work? Bas was totally convinced by his own logic because it fit Santiago's modus operandi so well . . . Yes, Alex may be the one pulling the trigger, but it was Santiago putting the gun in his hand.

But Bas wasn't going out without a fight.

Two days later, he came back to her with the perfect plan.

"We have to make Santiago think you are having an affair," he announced with a sneaky grin.

"Are you crazy? He'll—"

"With Alex," he cut her off and added, "if we put it in his head that it's Alex, he'll stop trusting Alex . . . he'll think twice about giving the family to him. Especially if he thinks Alex is trying to take over the family and avenge his father," Bas proposed.

Mel had to admit it was a great plan. Bas surprised her coming up with it. She had been looking at him as a common thug, but now she saw him in a different light as a thinker.

With pussy as a motivator, a nigguh will figure out how to crawl through a keyhole.

She wrapped her arms around his neck and pushed her tongue down his throat. "So . . . I see you plan to have it all." She smirked.

He gripped her ass lustfully. "Goddamn right!" he answered, because in the chess game he was playing, looking down at the queen was a job done.

He slid his hand under her skirt and the feel of her soft, juicy ass made him careless. They were standing in Santiago's living room.

"No," Mel weakly protested, even though the feel of his big hands palming her ass had her weak in the knees.

"Fuck that!" he growled, breathing hard and animalistic in her ear as he fingered her from the back. "Santiago ain't even in the city, and even if he was, even if he come in right now, I'll take whatever he would give for this moment with you." By the time he finished his statement, he had her skirt hiked up and her panties around her ankles. He lifted her right out of her panties.

"You want this pussy bad, don't you?" she huffed, wrapping her legs around his waist, riding his two fingers that he had buried deep up in her.

"Hell yeah!" he grunted, using his free hand to unbutton his jeans. He pulled out his big black dick and positioned her on the head. As soon as he began to penetrate her, Mel tried to scramble away.

"Oh my! Fuck! It's. Too. Bigggg!" she moaned as he filled her up, and he wasn't all the way in.

"This big dick feel great all up in your stomach, don't it?" he grunted.

"Ohhhh yessss!" she gasped, holding on to him tight and digging her nails in his neck.

When she finally got used to his size, it was like she couldn't stop cumming. Santiago always gave her multiple orgasms, but with Bas, her pussy felt like a fountain she came so many times. By the time he exploded inside her, she was exhausted with pleasure.

"Shit! That was good," she replied, trying to catch her breath.

"That's how it's gonna be from now on, baby . . . I promise," he vowed and the look in his eyes was the same one all those years back in the Chinese restaurant, so she knew she had him on lock.

Chapter 28

As Honest As Enemies

Pitch black...

That's all Bas could see through the black mask he had over his head. Combined with the fact that it was nighttime, Bas couldn't even make out the figures of the men seated around him in the van. He could only hear their voices as the van bumped along, making turns and abrupt stops.

"How much further?" Bas questioned.

"Don't worry about it," was the gruff reply.

He couldn't help but worry. Bas was surrounded by goons of the Rosario family. He half expected to not even make it to the destination at all and just get a bullet in his head.

Basim had requested a meeting with Chez Rosario by sending word through a chick he and Chez both had dealings with. Chez sent word back to be at a certain place at a certain time. He arrived and so did the van. They masked him up, dumped him inside, and then took off. Even though they were only fifteen minutes outside the city, it took them over an hour because the driver spent most of the time going in circles, making abrupt turns, and running red lights to make sure he shook any tails. They finally arrived.

When they took the hood off, Bas found that they were out in the middle of the woods. That really made him expect a bullet in the back of his head. He relaxed when the van door slid open and he saw Chez and Antonio standing in front of a Benz. The headlights provided illumination and two machine-gun-toting goons flanked both men. The goons from the van walked Bas over.

Chez looked him up and down. "Well, well, you actually showed. You gotta a lot of heart, Bas. I'll give you that." Chez smirked.

Bas looked around at all the ice grills, especially Antonio's. But they were warranted. The Rosario's were Santiago's sworn enemies, and he had called for a meeting to make a deal.

"It ain't heart that brought me here," Bas replied.

"Oh no? Then why are you here?" Chez questioned.

"Same reason you here. Mutual interest."

Chez nodded. "That remains to be seen. Speak your peace," Chez told him.

"Santiago. He's finished."

"How you figure?"

"'Cause I'ma finish 'im. Once I do, I call a truce. You can have the city if you give me your backing in all."

Antonio guffawed and spat. "Fuck outta here. It's a trick, yo," Antonio growled, pulling out his gun. "Let me blast this bitch ass nigguh!"

Chez gave him a cold look and silenced his brother. He looked back at Bas. "The youth. They'd rather act gangsta than be gangsta. Continue!"

"Believe me, this is no set up. It's time I spread my wings," Bas said.

"And you gonna what, murder Santiago? What about his team? You think they gonna just roll over?"

Bas shook his head. "Naw, but they won't be a factor. Once I convince Santiago they turned against him, he'll kill them himself."

Chez nodded and chuckled. "Divide and conquer."

"Exactly."

"Yeah, but he won't turn on Tariq. What about him?" Antonio questioned.

"I got a bitch on Tariq as we speak. He likes to get high too much. He'll be a crack head by the time she finished with him," Bas responded.

Chez couldn't help but laugh. "Goddamn, you a cold muhfucka. But if Santiago can't trust you, how can I?"

Bas shrugged and smirked. "You can't. That's why we'll get along just fine. We're as honest as enemies."

"Honest as enemies . . . I like that. I tell you what . . . you've got a deal if you take out Mr. Colon as well," Chez proposed.

Bas paused. He knew what Chez was doing. He wanted to kill two birds with one stone. Get rid of his biggest competitor and make Bas dependent on him for a connect. That way, Bas could never go to war with him.

"Well?" Chez smirked.

"Okay. You got a deal."

"Naw, Bas, you got a deal," Chez replied as they reached out and shook hands.

Satisfied with the outcome, Bas half-smiled and gently rubbed his hands together. He imagined himself standing on a pinnacle of the earth looking down at his subjects, those who were so easily controlled under his influence. Even a wise man like Santiago had unthinkingly fallen prey into Bas's trap.

The human mind is the strongest tool in the world, but it is also the easiest to manipulate. Once Bas planted the seed in Santiago's mind, it was nothing to water and cultivate until it blossomed into the statement, "I think Mel and Alex are having an affair."

Bas had combined Santiago's two weaknesses. His love for Mel and his guilt for Alex. Once the words hit

Santiago's ears, his initial reaction, his first thought was, *I deserve it.* He knew he had mistreated Mel for years and had murdered Alex's father. His guilt accepted it as true, but his ego made him resist. He turned to the bottle, just as Bas had anticipated, because it was what he did when he was stressed.

"Relax, Big Brah, you know you don't take alcohol well," Bas had warned, but his mind was really screaming, *Drink up, motherfucka, drink up!*

Bas watched Santiago pace the room, and from years of watching those wheels turn, he knew exactly which way they spun. He played Santiago like a finely tuned violin, making himself the interpreter of Santiago's reality. So when Santiago told him, "Keep this between us," Bas knew it was his ego talking. And whenever Bas followed Mel, it was for himself, not Santiago.

"Open the door, and you better be naked when I get in there," Bas said, the day he called Mel after following her to the motel.

"I already am, daddy. Just bring that big dick," she cooed back.

But the final touch was making sure Santiago was charged with Alex's murder. The reason Mel had been talking to Alex was to plan a surprise party for Santiago, or so Alex thought.

"That's why he can't know anything, Alex, so don't tell him we talk," Mel explained.

While Bas played Santiago, Mel played Alex.

"No problem, I got you," Alex replied.

After hanging up, Mel giggled. "No baby, I got you."

The night Alex died, Mel and Bas had choreographed it perfectly. She was to go to Alex's condo for last minute details. Santiago's birthday was a week away.

"When you come in, carry the spaghetti dish in your right hand, tell him you bought dinner," Bas had instructed.

When she entered Alex's home, she did just that.

"That's what's up. I was in this muhfucka about to starve." Alex chuckled.

Mel laughed. "Just like a bachelor."

"When you go to hand it to him, let it fall back against you. Catch it so the stain is in the middle of your dress," Bas had coached her.

She performed like a pro. "I'm . . . oh my god, it's all over me!" she gasped, looking down at her pasta-stained dress. "Where's your washer and dryer?"

"In the back," Alex told her.

Bas advised Mel, "Hopefully by then, Santiago will be there. Don't come out the back until you hear Santiago. Throw on any old shirt or whatever, just make sure you look like you've just finished fucking," Bas emphasized.

"Like this?" Mel had quipped, gripping Bas's dick as she lay naked beside him in bed.

"Just like this." He laughed.

"Yo, Mel, it's Santiago," Alex called out to her casually, right before he went to open the door.

When Alex opened the door and smiled, it wasn't to challenge or taunt Santiago, he was simply happy to see his cousin. He expected Mel to stay out of sight, but he knew she had emerged when the expression on Santiago's face went from stone cold to murderous rage. Alex glanced over his shoulder and saw what Santiago saw: Mel, dressed in his shirt and shorts, barefoot, looking like they had been fucking.

"Santiago has to see you, ma. That's the key. When he sees you, he won't think, he'll react," Bas predicted.

"You betrayed me!" Santiago exploded, unloading his whole clip in Alex.

"Wow!" Mel giggled, tickling Bas's chin. "You're so bad . . . you deserve to be the boss."

Bas's chest swelled with gaseous pride. "I am the boss."

"Then I guess that makes me the Boss Bitch." Mel grinned. They both laughed, basking in the afterglow of their stolen moment and the sudden collapse of the man they both feared and despised.

Chapter 29

Violence and Murder

After the rape, Eva just lay on the couch. Numb. She felt the ooze of Bas's sperm seeping out of her pussy and down the crack of her ass. She could still smell his musky scent all over her. In the background, *Columbiana* blasted with the sounds of Spanish, gunshots, and explosions. All around her, the nightmarish memory swirled, replaying itself in her head, thrust for sickening thrust.

You said you would never leave me. Eva sniffled.

I didn't, her conscience replied as always, in Spanish.

You said you would protect me.

I can't if you won't let me.

Let you?

Let me ... out.

Tears streamed down Eva's face as she shook her head. *No ... that's not who I want to be!*

Her inner self laughed mockingly. *Be? This is who we are!*

No! Eva protested, but then a strange thing happened.

She felt herself get up and head for the kitchen. Eva felt like she was playing a first person shooter video game she couldn't control. It was like her body had a mind of its own. She bent down to the cabinet under the sink, then took out the .380 Santiago kept holstered behind the pipes. She cocked it back.

What are you doing?

You want me to protect you? That's what I'm doing.

With that, she headed toward the master bedroom. Eva was powerless to protest. It was like the old folks said: "A witch riding your back when you can't move, even though you're awake." She felt exactly the same, except she was moving. Eva was just no longer controlling the moment. She walked in and found Bas and Mel in bed, sitting up kissing. When she entered, Bas broke the kiss, looked at her and smiled.

"Damn, lil mama, you want some mo' already?" he leered.

Stone faced, she raised the gun, and inside, Eva screamed, "Nooooo!"

Boc! Boc! Boc!

She moved swiftly and expertly. Two to the chest and one to the head. The look of painful surprise frozen on

Bas's face as his heart detonated in his chest and his brains volcanoed from the top of his dome. His body slumped sideways in Mel's lap. She screamed like a white bitch in a scary move, hands on her cheeks. Then Eva watched the gun swing over, aimed at her mother.

"Not my mother, too!"

"You can't shoot me! I'm your mother!" Mel yelled.

"Was."

Boc! Boc! Boc!

Eva sat up, bolted straight on the couch, chest heaving. She looked around to get her bearings. Once she did, she sighed in relief.

"It was only a nightmare," she mumbled into her hands.

But the rape hadn't been, which was evident from the dried cum on her inner thigh and the sickening smell of Bas still on her. She thought about the nightmare and she couldn't lie. Blowing Bas away felt so good she damn near came. Yet, she had to get a grip on her thoughts because eventually those same ideas became real actions. This *thing* inside her reeked of violence and murder and apathy—it had no conscience. Eva felt its strong magnetic pull. But it was a part of her she vowed to never let out . . . ever.

Chapter 30

Lucky Seven

The rain of bullets erupted from the passing van and made sure everybody on the block got wet with their own blood. A few tried to return fire, but only died hoping.

Except one.

Nazir.

Nazir was a block general for Tariq's squad on the north side of town, a lucrative area that brought in a lot of drug money. He was only seventeen, but Tariq liked him. He had a lot of heart, and being only 5-feet 8-inches, he had to have it.

When the van full of shooters came through, Nazir had been squatting down, playing dice. His lucky seven literally saved his life.

"Get 'em, girls! Ah!" he grunted, releasing the black dotted white cubes from his hand and watching them tumble end over end until they hit the wall and spun on three and four.

"Pay me, motherfuckas!" He laughed, then bent down to pick up his winnings.

Bbbbbrrrrrrrrrrppppp!

The automatic fire spat, opening the chest of the dude behind Nazir who became exposed when he bent over. The force of the bullets literally blew him out of one sneaker as his body flew to the ground. Two more went down before anyone could get off a single shot.

Nazir snatched his .40 from his waist and kicked off the safety with his thumb. At first he thought it was a drive by, but when he saw the van stop, he knew the shooters had come to put in work.

"Aaahhh!" He heard one dude scream as the bullet tore off chunks of his body before a single head shot put him out of his screaming misery.

Nazir arose from his squatting position, running and shooting at the same time.

Boc! Boc! Boc! Boosh!

Only one of his shots found a target and that was only the van's windshield. But when one of the shooters shot back, one of the bullets caught Nazir in the shoulder, knocking him off his feet.

"Fuck!" he agonized as he scrambled to get back up.

He didn't have time for pain because the shot had left him in the open. The shooter aimed to finish the job.

Nazir ran and dove over the hood of a car, shooting back the whole time. When he landed hard on the other side, his gun was empty, but he had hit the shooter dead in the chest. His dead body fell face first out of the van just as the van skidded off.

Hearing the skidding tires made Nazir roll over on his back with relief. Adrenaline pumping, he lay there leaking blood and thinking only one thing: Vindication.

"Fuckin' Rosario Brothers!" he growled.

If he only knew.

"Ow, goddamn!" Nazir bellowed, pulling away from the needle his sister was now using to stitch up his injury.

"Boy, quit hollerin' like a lil' bitch!" Kika huffed. "Unless you wanna go to the hospital!"

Nazir knew the hospital was out. The shootout would be all over the news. Besides, Kika was a registered nurse, so she knew how to dress and stitch up a clean-through bullet wound.

"Serves your ass right for bein' in them streets," she ranted, being extra careful with her work. "I done told you a million times, get a job! Go back to school! What you need is Jesus in your life!"

Nazir, gritting his teeth against the pain, replied through clenched teeth, "Kika, not now."

He knew she meant well, even if she got on his nerves. Ever since their mother had died when he was seven and Kika was fourteen, Kika had raised him. She worked two jobs and went to school, giving up her childhood just to keep them out of foster care. The only thing she found solace in was church.

Once Kika finished, she gave the wound a healthy slap, making Nazir jump out of the chair.

"A'ight girl! Don't make me fuck you up!"

"Fuck who up?" she asked playfully, throwing up her hands in her boxing stance. She was a big girl, about the size of Jennifer Hudson before the weight loss, but she wore it well.

Nazir ignored her playful taunt and snatched up his cell phone. He quickly scrolled to Bas's code name and number and sent the call.

"Yo Naz, what's good, lil' homie?" Bas greeted cheerfully.

"Shit is fucked up, unc. Them Rosario nigguhs getting bold as fuck," Nazir told him.

"I already heard. How you? You good? I heard you got hit."

"Naw, naw, I'm gucci."

"That's what's up. Where you at?"

"At the crib, yo. Man, we can't keep sittin'—"

Bas cut him off. "Ease off, lil homie. I know what's good. Don't worry, I'm on my way."

They hung up.

"Please, Nazir, this could be a sign. The Lord doesn't always call twice," Kika warned.

Nazir was only half-listening, because alarms were chiming in his head. Something seemed . . . off about the phone call. He couldn't put his finger on it, but he felt it. It was like having something stuck in his tooth, and it would annoy him until he worked it loose.

"Nazir, did you hear me?" Kika questioned.

"Huh?"

She sucked her teeth, irately. "You ain't heard a word I said."

"What, Kika?" he asked, knowing if he didn't respond she'd go on and on.

"Pray with me," she suggested with hopeful eyes.

Nazir swallowed his unbelief long enough to appease her emotions. They joined hands and bowed their heads.

"The Lord is my shepherd; I shall not want . . ." she began.

*****

Bas was summoning his own angels of death.

"He at the crib. Don't fuckin' miss this time," he hissed into the phone.

The driver of the van, now in a Pathfinder, nodded and hung up.

The shooters had only been a block away when Bas called. They pulled up outside Nazir's building.

*****

Why is he comin over here? Nazir questioned, his thoughts racing a mile a minute.

"Yea, though I walk through the valley of the shadow of death," Kika droned on.

I heard you got hit.

I heard you got hit.

I heard you got hit.

Those five words echoed across his mind. He kept rolling it over and over trying to figure out. *How did he know?*

"You prepare a table before me in the presence of my enemies . . ."

*****

The killers locked and loaded their automatic weapons as they mounted the stairs to the third floor apartment.

*****

Bas? Nazir thought.

Finding the answer to his question was like doing a math problem in his head over and over and coming up with the same answer, but it just didn't look right.

Knock! Knock! Knock!

"Amen."

"Yo!" Nazir called out.

Half a beat passed.

"Yeah," came the dry monotone from the other side of the door.

"Hol' up," Nazir replied as he crossed the room to get his gun off the coffee table.

Killers rarely have patience.

Bbbrrrraaapppp!

The automatic weapon thundered through the small apartment, sending door splinters everywhere.

"Oh my God!" Kika screamed.

Nazir aimed at the door as the two shooters tried to kick in the door, but his gun was empty. "Shit!" he swore, remembering he had emptied the clip earlier.

He grabbed Kika's hand and took off for the back bedroom, just as the shooters kicked in the door. The gunfire barely missed them as they dipped into the room, slamming the door behind them.

Nazir threw up the window and pushed Kika to the fire escape on the other side.

"Go, ma, hurry up!" he urged.

Bbrrrraaaap!

The gunfire turned the bedroom door into Swiss cheese. Kika scrambled out with Nazir right behind her. They jetted up the fire escape just as the shooters appeared in the window. The shots ricocheted and sparked off the metal of the fire escape as Nazir and Kika made their getaway. When they hit the next landing, Nazir kicked in the window and hurriedly cleared the glass.

"Come on, Ki! Go!"

He practically shoved her through the window then tumbled through after her. When he looked up, they were in a bedroom where an old man and a big-tittied young girl were on the bed butt naked and wide-eyed from the surprise entrance.

"Police, yo!" Nazir barked, scrambling up and running off.

The old man and young girl took off running, too. Nazir and Kika shot out of the front door. They ran to one of Nazir's jump offs' apartment and banged on the door.

"Nazir, what—what just happened?" Kika gasped, her heartbeat quickening.

Before he could answer, a short, thick red bone threw the door open, carrying a baby on her hip.

"Nazir? What if my husband—" she began to protest, but he pushed Kika and himself inside, then slammed the door behind them.

He barely heard her over the rage in his mind. *Bas*, he fumed, this time without the question mark.

It was clear to him that Bas had flipped sides. Now, it was time to even the score. "Thanks," he mumbled, unsure if Kika's prayer or those lucky sevens had saved them.

Chapter 31

Nina

E-vee . . . E-vee, baby . . . come on, ma, open the door. How you say it in Spanish? Abra, aba, some shit like that." Bas chuckled as he tried to turn the knob to Eva's locked door. "Don't be like this, lil ma. I know you liked it. The way you came all over my dick . . . Twice." Bas gripped himself, feeling himself harden.

"Umph, that pussy was tight. I can't wait to get you and your mama in the bed together for some family time." He laughed.

Eva shivered. She sat on her bed, knees pulled up to her chest, rocking back and forth. She had been locked in her room all day since she heard Bas come in. He banged on the door and made her jump.

"Eva! Stop playin' with me and open the door," Bas bassed, his rock hard dick making him impatient. "If I have to break it down, you'll be sorry," he sang in a mocking manner.

Eva began to sob.

"I'ma go fuck the shit out of yo' mama, and when I come back, if this door ain't open and you ain't butt naked on the bed, then I'ma teach you a lesson you'll never forget," he threatened.

Eva listened to his receding footsteps on the hardwood floor, feeling a strange mix of relief and mounting fear. She was in a panic. Her life seemed to be spiraling out of control. Everything was topsy-turvy. She couldn't stand to face the future that her mind was telling her was awaiting her. Death would be better.

Death.

The decision to commit suicide isn't one you think about, it's something you just do. It is not a solution, it is the only solution. At that moment, death called out to Eva like a magnet to metal. Had she had a gun, she wouldn't have hesitated to blow her own brains out. Eva jumped off the bed and headed to the bathroom.

"Lord, forgive me, but if you can't save me, please don't blame me for saving myself," she prayed between sobs.

She snatched open the medicine cabinet, looking for something, anything to put her out of her misery, but she found nothing that would do the job. Frustrated, she slammed the cabinet and looked at herself in the mirror.

"I hate you! I hate you! Why don't you just die?" she bellowed, slamming both fists against the cabinet. She dislodged the flimsy wooden box into the sink, shattering the mirror into jagged pieces.

One particularly sharp piece winked up at her, reflecting her image back at her. She picked it up and climbed into the empty tub. She gripped the glass, then turned her right wrist up.

"It's the only way," she mumbled, then winced as the cool, razor-sharp edge bit into her skin and blood ran free.

Eva dropped the glass, feeling a soothing sensation taking over, like all her burdens were seeping away like the blood in her veins. Her eyes fluttered, the tears fell, and she began to drift . . .

Suddenly, a pair of hands wrapped around her throat. Her eyes popped open, and she looked into the face of . . .

Herself?

Eva couldn't believe her eyes, but she was clearly looking at herself choking her other self to death. She would've thought it was a dream, but she could feel the cold, slender fingers squeezing the life out of her. She clawed at her own hands, desperately trying to loosen the grip.

"Oh, now you want to live, eh?" The other Eva laughed.

Eva kicked and thrashed, but the bolder, stronger Eva had her pinned.

"I'm sorry, ma-ma . . . but this is the only way," she told the fragile Eva.

It was the last thing she heard before Eva got totally weak and stopped clawing, stopped struggling, and eventually . . . leapt up from the tub and looked around. She was all alone.

She smiled. The Eva who was not Eva looked down at her bleeding wrist.

"The bitch couldn't even kill herself right." She snickered, eyeing the blood running down her arm.

The slice across her wrist was deep enough to bleed profusely but not deep enough to severe the vein. She got out of the tub, then wrapped a towel around her wrist tightly. Glancing in the sink, she picked up another jagged edge, admiring herself in it.

"Goddamn, you sexy," she purred, fluffing her hair with a giggle.

She held the broken glass in one hand and pulled her oversized T-shirt over her head with the other, leaving herself completely naked as she entered her bedroom. She dropped the shirt as she went, unlocked her bedroom door, and came back and lay on the bed. Bunching the pillow up behind her head and keeping both hands under the pillow, she rested spread eagle.

Several minutes later, she heard his approaching footsteps.

"Now we play my game," she whispered with a smirk.

The doorknob turned and Bas entered wearing nothing but his boxers and a lecherous grin. "I'm glad to see you came to your senses," he remarked.

"No . . . I just came," she retorted playfully, lifting her leg to reveal the juices glistening on her inner thigh.

Bas pulled his massive meat from his boxers and began squeezing it lustfully as he approached. "I knew you wanted this, you filthy fuckin' tease."

Seductively she bit her bottom lip and nodded, all the while watching him with the eyes of a panther. Bas slid up between her legs, licking along her calf and thigh. He ran his tongue along the lips of her pussy, lapping up the excess juices and making her squirm.

"Mmmm, don't tease me, daddy. Just gimme that great big dick," she groaned.

Bas lifted up, positioning his dick to penetrate. Without warning, she wrapped her legs around his back tightly and flipped him over until she was sitting on top of him. One hand she kept pressed on his forehead, and the other gripped the piece of glass she had to his throat. When Bas realized what she had to his neck, he flinched.

"Bit—"

"Uh uh uhhhn, I wouldn't do it if I were you," she sang sweetly, the whole time rolling her hips on his rock-hard dick. "The jugular is extremely vulnerable once it's punctured . . ." She shook her head.

Heated, Bas was fuming. This young bitch had the nerve to threaten him, but the feeling of her wet pussy gyrating on his shaft had his head fucked up. It was like being hot and cold at the same time just like she knew it would.

"You know what I'm about to do? I'm fixin' to shave mister," she sang in a syrupy southern drawl that had Bas instantly thinking of *The Color Purple*.

"Bitch, you crazy!" he spat.

She smirked. "No, I'm serious. Don't ever threaten me again. Whatever you gonna do, just do it, but the next time you threaten me, you better kill me," she warned, looking him dead in his eyes.

Bas was not a man who knew fear, so he was far from scared. But he could see that she was definitely serious.

"You—" he started to say. But she smothered his mouth with a suffocating kiss, as if she was trying to suck the air from his lungs, while at the same time she shifted her hips and rocked back, taking every inch of his huge dick.

"Fuck!" he grunted, because her pussy felt so good when he felt her contracting walls.

"Oh, you like that, baby? Huh? Tell me you like that," she panted, bouncing on his dick, hard and steady.

"Hell yeah, I like it," Bas exclaimed, gripping her hips and guiding her into every thrust.

She leaned back, grabbing his thighs then pulling her legs from under her so she was squatting on his dick. The sensation of the move shot electric bolts all through his body, curling his toes. No bitch had rode his dick so well, it damn near had his eyes rolled up in the back of his head.

With a snarl in her lip, she watched him. She took her foot and ran it along his chest then across his lips. He opened his mouth and began sucking her big toe.

"Oh shit, I'm about to bust!" he howled, fucking faster and faster, bouncing her harder and harder until he exploded. His body shuddered with chills.

"Goddamn, Eva, that pussy like gold!"

She smiled as she shifted, putting her legs back under her and leaning forward, until her lips brushed his.

"Don't call me that . . . call me by my middle name," she cooed, still squeezing her pussy muscles around his semi-erect dick.

Every squeeze made him convulse in the pelvis.

"Shit, chill, chill, chill . . . what's your middle name?"

"Nina."

"Nina," he echoed with a satisfied smile. His eyes fluttered shut, and his head got heavy on her pillow. Before he knew it, he was out.

Nina smiled and got off him. She headed out the door and down the hallway, ass jiggling. Once she came to her mother's door, she knocked, and then opened it to find Mel sitting up on the bed watching TV.

Mel's mouth dropped at the sight of Nina standing in her doorway.

"Please come and get your man out of my bed . . . he doesn't want to leave," Nina said with a sassy smirk, before turning and walking away.

Chapter 32

Rejection

As soon as Santiago laid eyes on Tariq, his heart dropped. He was as skinny as a pole. He stood in the front of the dorm, glued to the spot.

"You okay?" Mercedes asked, standing behind him.

"Yeah . . . yeah . . . I appreciate this," he remarked, because she had made sure he got in the same dorm with his son.

"Mm hmm, we'll see how much later," she quipped, walking away.

Santiago stared at Tariq, and Tariq could see the disappointment in his eyes. His father hurt him to his heart, because his gaze felt like rejection.

"Hey, Pop," Tariq said, trying to break the tension.

When he approached, Tariq wrapped him up in a tight hug. Santiago hugged him back, but even in his hug he could feel the disappointment.

"Walk me to my cell," Santiago said.

Tariq grabbed the green plastic mat and carried it to Santiago's cell. As they walked, several individuals called out to Santiago just to be heard talking to him. But Santiago didn't respond. He was in a zone. When they got to the cell, Tariq put the mat on the steel bunk and unrolled it.

"I see you got a thick one. My shit thin like them green high school gym mats," Tariq cracked, trying to make small talk.

"Close the door," Santiago told him, voice calm. Too calm.

Tariq knew his father well, so before he could even start, he tried to head him off. After he closed the door, he quickly blurted out, "Pop, I know I fucked up. I know. But . . . seeing that nigguh or . . . thinkin' it was the nigguh, my temper got the best of me."

"What happened?" Santiago asked in Spanish.

"I just told—"

"What . . . *happened!*" Santiago gritted.

Tariq dropped his head, because he now knew what he was referring to. "Pop, I . . . I . . ."

Santiago slammed his palm on the wall. "Don't fuckin' lie to me! What happened to turn you into a fuckin' addict?"

Tariq bristled. "I'm not no addict."

"Oh no?" Santiago growled, biting his bottom lip. "Look!" He grabbed Tariq by the back of the neck and snatched him in front of the mirror, forcing him to look at himself. Tariq didn't want to face the truth staring back at him, but Santiago forced him.

"Look!" Santiago barked again.

Tariq eyed his reflection. His cheeks were sunk in along with his eye sockets. He looked like the pipe had literally sucked the life out of him.

Santiago released him with a jerk. Tariq covered his face.

"I don't know what's happening to me!" he cried. "So much on my fuckin' mind, I couldn't think straight, man! I'm sorry . . . I'm sorry!" Tariq cried while Santiago stared at his bowed head coldly.

When he couldn't take any more, he slapped the shit out of Tariq, knocking him back on the bed. "You disgust me!" Santiago spat venomously. "You allow the world to make you weak, then you think cryin' like a baby makes you strong. You think I should pity you? You get nothing! You're a disgrace. There's no way you can run this family!"

Santiago's words hurt worse than the slap. Every syllable, every sentence made Tariq feel small. And no man ever wants to be belittled, even if his belittler is his own father.

Tariq laughed hysterically, tears still streaming down his cheeks. "Family? Family? Ha ha, what family? What family do we have left? You think I don't know? Huh?"

Santiago looked at him strangely, then his brow unfurled with understanding. He sighed. "That couldn't be helped. Murk, B, and Smoke had become . . . compromised. I had no choice," Santiago explained.

Tariq stood up from the bunk, feeling emboldened by the moral weight of his words. "I'm not talking about them bastards. I know. I was there. I'm talkin' about Alex."

"Alex?" Santiago echoed.

Tariq shook his head. "You can't lie to me any more than I can lie to you. You killed him, Pop. You killed your own blood! How can you talk to me about family?" Tariq accused.

Santiago's first thought was, *How did he know? Did Mel tell him? Bas?* He quickly shook off Bas, thinking his main man wouldn't spill the beans, and settled on Mel.

"Did your mother tell you that?"

"It doesn't matter who told me, the point is I know!" Tariq shot back.

Santiago paced a couple of steps then turned back to him. "This is not the time or the place to discuss this, okay? These walls have ears."

Tariq nodded smugly. "That says it all right there!"

His attitude irked Santiago, and he exploded. "No! You know what says it all? Weakness! Weak ass motherfuckas who think being my blood will hide their weakness!" Santiago boomed, pointing in Tariq's face. "But I don't give a fuck who it is, blood won't love you if you a weak ass nigguh. I. Don't. Care. Who. It. Is!"

There was no mistaking Santiago's tone or the look in his eyes. It both scared and angered Tariq. The rejection hung. He felt like the devil being tossed from the garden by God, and he reacted accordingly.

"I hear you, Pop . . . I hear you loud and clear," he replied.

Father and son eyed each other hard, then Tariq walked out.

Chapter 33

Sinking Fast

O h my Jesus! What are we going to do?" Kika ranted.

She and Nazir were in a hotel room on the outskirts of the city. Nazir peeped out of the curtain like Malcolm X. He held a .45 in his hand, while Kika sat on the bed with her hands nervously twittering in her lap.

"Everything's gonna be cool, Kiki," Nazir assured, calling her by the nickname he gave her.

Kika jumped off the bed. "Don't Kiki me, nigguh! Ain't nothin' cool! I told you those streets were like quicksand; once you get in you can't get out! Now look at us, sinkin' fast!"

"I'ma take care of this, okay? You just gotta take a few sick days until I do," he replied.

"I can't just take off, Nazir! You just gonna have to go to the police!"

He shot her a crazed glare. "The police? What the fuck are you talkin' about?"

"Nazir, please! Somebody tried to kill you! It ain't about snitchin'. It's about survivin'!" she reminded him.

Nazir spazzed.

"Look ma, I ain't going to the police. I ain't goin' to church, and I damn sure ain't goin' to no gaddamn Jesus! Those were real bullets. They were shooting at us, do you understand? Nobody can save us but us!" he bassed.

The clarity of his logic and the force of his words didn't make Kika agree with him, but she couldn't argue either. She folded her arms across her chest. "You didn't have to use the Lord's name in vain," she replied.

Seeing that he had hurt her, his whole mood softened. He took her by the arms gently and looked her in the eyes.

"Listen, Ki. I'm sorry, okay? I didn't mean to go that hard. Shit is crazy right now. I know you believe. I know you have faith in me right now, okay?"

She looked at him for an extra beat, nodded, then her face broke into an amused smile.

"What?" Nazir asked.

"How you gonna be my protector now? Seems like just yesterday I was pullin' Fat Tammy off your ass!"

They laughed.

"Naw, that don't count. That bitch was like six-two, 450 pounds in the third grade! Shit, you might still have to pull her off my ass now!"

Kika laughed to tears.

He stroked her cheek and gave her a dimpled grin. "See? That's what I like to see, you laughin'. I'll be back, okay?"

"Okay."

He started to walk out.

"Nazir."

He looked back.

"Faith ain't all I got." She smiled.

He winked and walked out.

Nazir had been trying to get at Tariq, but once the phone went from just ringing to saying not in service, he headed to the only place he knew he could get word to Tariq.

Cookie's crib.

He knew Cookie was Tariq's ride or die chick. He didn't know about her and Tariq being arrested. All he knew was Tariq was like a big brother to him, and even though he had never met him face to face, Santiago was an OG he looked up to and respected. He pulled his '08 BMW up to Cookie's building and got out, keeping his eyes peeled. He kept his hand on the butt of his pistol as he went inside.

Of course the elevator didn't work, so he had to take the stairs two at a time to the eighth floor.

"Goddamn, I got to work out." He chuckled, winded from the sixteen flight climb. He walked down the hall to the apartment on the end and knocked.

A few seconds later, he heard, "Who is it?"

"Nas."

"Who? I don't know you," she replied, obviously looking at him through the peep hole.

"I know. I'm looking for Tariq. Call him, he'll vouch for me," Nas assured her.

Nazir heard the bolts of the locks sliding and clunking free. She opened the door, and Nazir had to hold his tongue. *What the fuck happened to you?* he wanted to say.

Cookie was still sexy, but she had lost weight, and her eyes had the shifty gaze of a crack head. Nazir couldn't believe his eyes.

"What you want Tariq for?" she snapped.

"Is he here? I need to holla at him," Nas answered.

"No. What you need to holla at him about?" she probed.

He really wanted to curse her nosy ass out, but he respected Tariq too much, so he took a deep breath and replied, "Just tell him I came by."

"You got a number he could reach you at?"

"Yeah . . . 555–3811."

"Mm–hmm," Cookie said, looking him up and down. How old are you anyway? Anybody ever tell you, you look like Nas?"

He smirked, thinking, *Has anybody told you, you look a hot mess?*

"Naw," he lied, knowing he got that all the time.

"You holdin'?"

"Naw yo, just tell Tariq I came though."

"If I remember," she retorted, rolling her eyes and slamming the door.

*****

Once Naz left, Cookie grabbed her phone and speed dialed Bas. He answered on the third ring.

"Yo."

"Daddy, this Cookie. You said to call you if anybody come looking for Tariq, right?"

"Yeah, who was it?"

"I don't know his name. The young boy Tariq deal with, the one that look like the rapper Nas," Cookie explained.

"Nas."

"That's what I just said."

"Naw, that's his name."

"I know."

"Never mind," Bas growled.

Cookie shrugged it off.

"So when am I gonna see you?" Cookie cooed, her pussy getting wet just thinking about it.

At first, she didn't even pay Bas much attention, but when he caught her one night at the Vortex club, ten minutes later he had her climbing the bathroom stall trying to get away from that monster between his legs. Ever since then, she craved their side thing.

For Bas, she was strictly a means to an end. Since Tariq liked to get high, he wanted Cookie to put him on the high hardest to come down from—a crack high. Now that she had accomplished that, she was useless to him.

"When I can get away."

"I can't wait." She laughed.

Bas hung up. "I can," he said aloud, wondering what to do with dead weight AKA Cookie.

Chapter 34

Another Man's Lies

B as dialed another number, and as he waited for it to ring, Mel walked into the bedroom. "I need to talk to you," she huffed, folding her arms over her breasts.

He held up his finger as someone picked up.

"What's good, unc?"

"Yo, that nigguh was just over Cookie's house. I want y'all to go over there, have her call him back, and tell him Tariq on his way. You know what to do when he get there," Bas instructed.

"What about her? I ain't tryin' to do no dirt around that triflin' bitch."

"Fuck it, kill her too then. I don't give a fuck. Just don't miss this time," Bas warned.

"We on it."

Bas hung up. He wanted to make sure all Santiago's loyal soldiers were dead. Especially Nazir. He was young but fiercely loyal and a cold-blooded killer. Bas knew Nas wasn't in a position to be a thorn in his side, but he was definitely a pebble in his shoe.

He turned to Mel.

"Stay away from Eva, Bas. I don't want you fucking her anymore," Mel warned.

"Come on, ma. It ain't that serious. I'm just havin' a little fun." He tried to grab her around the waist, but she pulled away.

"Yeah, well, you've had your fun. Dead it," she hissed.

At first, she didn't care about Bas raping her own daughter. A part of her wanted Eva to feel pain, to know what life was about (was the way Mel put it). But now it seemed as if Bas was paying more attention to Eva, and that, she wasn't having.

She was also upset with herself for believing another man's lies. Why did men always do that? At first, it's all sweet, all promises and dreams . . . until they get what they want. Mel just wanted to be loved and not lied to. Her heart cried out, *Is that too much to ask?*

Bas pulled her close and kissed her gently. "You ain't got nothin' to worry about, baby. I'm forever addicted to this chocolate," he crowed softly, running his tongue from her ear to her collar bone.

His caressing kisses felt so sweet, even though deep down she knew they came from a lying tongue. But Mel desperately wanted to believe that she hadn't made a mistake. That she hadn't helped a man whom she loved for a man that didn't love her. She knew there was a big difference; she just hoped she made the right decision.

Bas pulled the sash of her silk robe, letting it fall open as he sank to his knees, kissing her bare stomach.

"Ohhhh," she sighed softly, eyes fluttering like butterfly wings.

He cocked her leg up on his shoulder, pulling her panties aside and wrapping his lips around her clit.

"Oh fuck!" she cooed, back arched up against the wall.

Bas slid two of his massive fingers inside her pussy while he sucked and nibbled on her swollen clit. She gripped his ears, pulling his head into her, her mind gaga over the tongue action that had her pussy about to explode.

"Oh, Bas, I'm about to cum!"

"Cum for me, baby. Cum all over my tongue," he urged, the vibration of his words feeling like a vibration on her clit.

That's all Mel needed, throwing her head back and releasing her nectar all over his mouth and chin.

"Damn, you taste so good," Bas remarked, but in his mind it wasn't Mel he was tasting . . .

It was Nina.

Vindicated Love

Chapter 35

Not a Game

Nina sat on Asia's bed, going through the music on her iPhone while she showered. She came out wearing a towel and headed to her panty drawer.

"I didn't know you like Sade," Nina remarked.

"My mom plays her all the time. I love her lyrics. They're deep," Asia replied.

Nina cocked her head to the side, quizzically. "Asia, what are you eating? You getting fat." She giggled.

"No I'm not, you're just a hater." Asia waved her off dismissively.

Nina got off the bed and came over to her. "No, for real, come here. Look for yourself." Nina took her by the hand and led her in front of the full-length mirror on the back of her door.

"Look."

"At what?"

"At you. Take off the towel."

Asia looked over her shoulder at Nina strangely.

"For what?"

"So you can see for yourself . . . girl. Please, we've seen each other naked a million times," Nina reminded her.

Asia hesitated and untucked the towel and let it fall to the floor. She stood in the mirror butt naked, golden brown and juicy.

"See?" Nina remarked triumphantly.

"See what?"

"Look at these hips." Nina playfully slapped her hip.

"Girl!" Asia laughed, taking a swipe at her that she easily avoided.

"I'm serious," Nina replied, standing behind her in the mirror. She pinned Asia with a mesmerizing gaze as her smile faded.

"I'm sayin' . . . it's not a bad thing. I mean, it looks good on you, all this jiggle," Nina commented, her lips close to Asia's ears.

Asia slightly trembled, but it was like she couldn't look away from Nina's eyes, as Nina slowly guided her hands over her hips.

"You really are beautiful, Asia? But you fucked up, didn't you? You got in over your head and now the tide's dragging you out to sea . . . out to me," Nina whispered in Spanish.

Asia giggled nervously. "What are you saying?"

Nina smiled at her through the mirror, replying in English, "Just saying how beautiful they are, that's all!" Her caress ended at the top of her thighs, right under her young, plump ass cheeks. Nina walked around her, leaning against the mirror, openly admiring Asia's body.

"You're . . . different," Asia said, because Nina's gaze made her feel nervous and excited at the same time.

"Different how?"

"I don't know . . . darker?"

Nina laughed. "I must've got a tan, huh?" She broke the spell by walking back over to the bed.

Asia went and put on her panties.

"You wanna have some fun?" Nina asked.

"Shit, you already know the answer to that question!"

They both laughed.

"Can you get your mother's car?"

"Yeah probably. Why?"

Nina smiled mischievously, biting the corner of her lip. "Get the keys and I'll show you."

"Are you sure?" Asia asked, her voice filled with uncertainty.

Within twenty minutes, they were sitting outside Kim's large house. The streetlights beamed down on them, giving Nina's face the illusion of being half in the light and half in the darkness.

"Yeah, we're just going to scare her up, that's all. Make her regret all that mean shit she did to me," Nina replied.

"I'm pretty sure she already does after that ass whoopin' you put on her," Asia quipped.

"Come on, ma," Nina purred, running her fingertip along Asia's cheek. "Don't you trust me?"

When a person can't be trusted, but they feel guilty about it, they try to over compensate in diverse ways. Asia's way was to try to show Nina she really was her BFF.

"Don't get carried away," Asia remarked as she opened the door.

"I'm not—" Nina mumbled, opening hers at the same time. "You are."

The two of them walked up the walkway and knocked. It didn't take long before Kim threw open the door. Carelessly she held a phone between her ear and shoulder, saying, "Damn, Trish, you got here—"

She froze like a bitch when she saw who it was. Her heart pounded in her chest, but she refused to show it.

"Let me call you back," Kim said, hanging up. "What do you want?"

"Truce." Nina smiled sweetly. "I'm really sorry about everything that happened. Please, just hear me out."

Kim folded her arms over her chest. "I'm listenin'."

"Can I come in? I promise I won't be long."

Kim felt emboldened by the fact that she was in her own house, and Trish was on the way. She stepped aside to allow them in, but still giving Nina attitude.

"Hi, Mrs. Hathaway!" Nina yelled in the general direction of the back of the house.

Kim closed the door. "My mother's not at home. Now, tell me what you want," she insisted.

"I just wanted to say, I'm really sorry . . ." Nina began sweetly, but in mid-sentence she pulled a .32 snub from her waist, "for not killing you the first time!"

She grabbed Kim by the hair and proceeded to pistol whip her face into a bloody pulp.

Asia covered her face and screamed into her hands. "Oh my God, Eva! Please stop! Please stop!"

"You thought you were over, didn't you, bitch? Huh! Talk that shit now!" Nina huffed, pulverizing Kim.

Kim was barely clinging to consciousness when Nina released the grip on her hair, and she fell into a lump at her feet.

"You're gonna kill her!" Asia cried.

Nina looked at her. "No I'm not . . . you are," she said without a trace of a smile, holding out the bloody gun to her.

Asia's eyes exploded. "What?"

"Take the gun, Asia."

"Are you crazy?"

"Maybe. But you're gonna take this damn gun."

"P-p-please," Kim croaked from the floor, pulling on Nina's pant leg.

Nina kicked loose.

"I'm not doin' that, Eva! I'm leaving!" Asia backed away.

"No, you misunderstood, bitch. You don't have a choice!" Nina spat, pulling a small .25 revolver from the small of her back. She aimed it straight in Asia's face. "Now take the fuckin' gun!"

The crazed look in Nina's eyes let Asia know that this was definitely not a game.

"Why–why are you doing this?" Asia screamed, almost hysterical.

Filled with fury, Nina slapped her with her free hand. "Bitch, calm down! You know, I wondered when I looked back over the past couple of weeks: Why is this bitch askin' so many questions about my family? I couldn't put my finger on it . . . that is, until I put my finger on your phone. Remember when you were in the shower?"

When Nina mentioned her phone, Asia's stomach dropped. She knew she was cold busted.

"I can tell by your expression you know where I'm goin' with this. Beep! This is Detective Mulligan returning your call. Just wanted to say that information you gave us on Tariq checked out. When can we meet again? Let me know. Beep!" Nina said, doing her best white girl impression. "Now . . . you wanna talk about puttin' in work? Then you about to put in your own."

Asia trembled with fear. "Eva, I'm sorry. They set me up. They said if I didn't tell, I was going to jail. I swear I was just trying to help Tariq and they arrested me! Please don't make me do this!"

Eva put the gun to her temple. "I'm through talkin'! Kill her, or I'ma kill you," she warned, cocking back the hammer. The metallic click seemed to ricochet all through Asia's body.

Reaching out her shaking hand, Asia took the gun. The bloody handle was warm and sticky. She looked down at Kim.

"Don't kill me. Please!" she strained to beg.

"Five, four, three, two . . ." Nina counted down, but before she reached one, Asia pulled the trigger.

Boom!

The bullet hit Kim in the throat, making her gag for air.

"Again!" Nina demanded.

Boom!

The bullet struck Kim in the cheek, blowing out her eye socket, yet she still squirmed.

"Goddamn, will you kill that bitch already? Put the gun to her forehead!"

Asia did, closing her eyes and pulling the trigger.

Splat!

The blast split Kim's wig, and she moved no more. Nina looked at Asia and smiled. "Welcome to the family."

Asia dropped the gun and put her hands to her face, inadvertently smearing blood on her cheeks.

"Oh my God! What have I done?" She sobbed, looking at Kim's lifeless body leaking blood in the carpet.

Nina dashed to the kitchen and came back with a loaf of bread, dumping the bread as she walked. She picked up the gun with the bag, then held the bag up for Asia to see.

"Do you know what I have in the bag?"

"Th–the gun?"

"No, the murder weapon. With your fingerprints on it. You no longer work for the police, you work for me. I own you. Are we clear?"

Asia nodded, tears streaming.

"Good, let's go."

The chiming doorbell froze them both. They looked at each other. It chimed again.

"Kim, hurry up, girl. I gotta pee!" Trish urged.

"Get over there, out of sight," Nina ordered Asia.

Asia did as she was told.

Nina tiptoed behind the door and turned the knob with the corner of her shirt to avoid leaving fingerprints.

The door opened, and Trish walked in wearing her Beats headphones, singing along to Beyoncé. She had her eyes closed, so into the note she was trying to hit, but when she opened them, the last thing she saw was Kim's dead body.

Boc! Boc! Boc!

Nina stepped from behind the door and put three shots in the back of Trish's head. She never saw it coming. When she fell on her face, Nina stood over her and put two more in the base of her skull.

Boc! Boc!

"I hate these lil' shits!" Nina cursed, referring to the small caliber gun. "Let's go!"

As they ran out, Asia took one last look at the scene. She had come in a snitch, but she was leaving a murderer. She shuddered to think what the future held.

Chapter 36

Survival

Acevedo, shut up! You got a visit!" the officer bellowed.

Santiago smiled to himself, because in his mind it could only be one person.

Eva.

He had been trying to call Eva but got no answer. He hadn't seen her since the night he got shot and arrested, so he worried that the ordeal may have left her traumatized.

"Yo, play my game for me," he told a dude standing near.

The dude took the cards from Santiago, who made his way to the door. He pulled his jumpsuit up from being bunched around his waist to up on his shoulders.

As soon as he was led out, Tariq got up and headed straight for the phones. He picked up the receiver, unballed a piece of paper he had palmed in his hand, and dialed the written number.

She accepted the collect call once she heard who it was. "I see you thought about my offer," Melissa remarked, as soon as the call connected.

"Yeah, yeah, baby. I think about you all the time." He smiled into the phone, trying to give the impression he was talking to a girlfriend.

Melissa snickered. "Next, I guess you'll want to know what I'm wearing."

"That would be nice."

"Handcuffs. But I promise not to use 'em on you if you're ready to deal."

Tariq looked around nervously, stomach twisting over what he was about to do. Never did he think he'd even contemplate being a snitch, but his father's rejection both hurt and scared him. It was ironic that the very reason Santiago didn't tolerate addicts was because of what Tariq was contemplating doing. But Tariq didn't see the irony. He only saw survival.

"Time's ticking. You know how quick these calls are," she reminded him.

"Yeah yo, I'm . . . I'm ready."

"Good choice."

"But not while I'm in here," he added quickly. "Pop got eyes and ears all over."

"I'll take care of that."

"And yo . . . you said—you said you was gonna look out," Tariq reminded her sheepishly.

The past few nights, he had been tossing and turning, unable to sleep. The monkey was on his back hard. Especially after he thought he smelled somebody on his tier smoking crack in the wee hours. He needed to scratch his itch.

"You're gonna have to be a real good boy for that, Tariq," she taunted him, enjoying her power over him.

"Whateva yo, just make it happen," he gruffed, then hung up and slunk back to his cell.

*****

Santiago had entered the visitation room. It was simply a row of phones on both sides of the room. On the other side of the extra thick Plexiglas there were more phones for the visitors. Everything was in the open. No privacy. Santiago scanned the unfamiliar faces, his heart falling when he didn't spot Eva waving for him. Instead, a young boy who bore a striking resemblance to the rapper Nas was waving him over. Santiago scowled, then looked over his shoulder to make sure no one was behind him. The young boy pointed at Santiago and waved again. Reluctantly, Santiago walked over and picked up the phone but didn't sit down.

"Who you?"

"I'm Nazir, yo, a friend of Tariq's," he replied.

Santiago clenched and unclenched his jaw. Just hearing his son's name had him on the edge.

"Yeah well, I don't know you," he retorted, then started to hang up.

"It's Bas, unc," Nazir said quickly, seeing he was losing Santiago. "I think he sour."

Santiago snatched the phone back to his ear. "What the fuck you just say?"

"Man, Bas did—"

Santiago had to fight from spazzing on this little nigguh and letting everyone in his business. "Look here, lil' nigguh. I don't know who the fuck you are, but I can damn sure find out! Don't fuckin' come at me wit' no bullshit!"

Nazir didn't like anybody yelling at him, no matter who they were. His motto was a man only dies once; a coward dies a thousand times. But he bit his tongue because he knew telling Santiago about his man wouldn't go down easy.

"Ay yo, you think I'd come down here to waste your time and mine for some bullshit? Bas was like a fuckin' uncle to me, so believe me, I'm fucked up, too!"

Santiago glared at Nazir, and even though Nazir didn't return the hard gaze, he definitely didn't look away.

"Say what you came to say," Santiago snarled out, after a tense thirty seconds.

"I'm sayin', you know we on these phones, but feel me, a'ight? So yeah, I was on the block when a rack of nigguhs came through on some Rambo shit. You wit' me?" Nazir asked.

"I'm listenin."

"So boom, nigguhs lit shit up like the Fourth. Left everybody leakin' for real, ground zero. Shit was crazy, but of course them bitch ass nigguhs missed the God."

Santiago couldn't help but crack a slight grin.

"I went to the crib and I'm buggin! I'm thinkin' it was the Roaches," he said, using the derogatory term for the Rosario family. "So you know I'm ready to go all out! So I hit unc up and tell him what went down. He . . . he ain't sound right. Wasn't no type of concern in 'im; he was calm as fuck—on some, 'where you at' type shit. I told 'im and ain't think nothin' of it 'cause this unc, feel me? Three minutes later, muhfuckas bring it to me at my door! Shit is crazy! How the fuck they know if he ain't tell 'em?"

Santiago listened intently, taking in every word. He could definitely see Nazir's point, but he didn't start to think until Nazir added, "I don't know what the fuck is goin' on! First Murk, then like seven shot callers on the west side, two more on the east. It's like the fuckin' Roaches takin' out our whole team."

Santiago scowled and leaned forward.

"What did you say?"

"It's like they—"

"Naw, what about the shot callers?"

"What, you ain't know? They found like seven of 'em dead!"

I didn't push their button, Santiago thought. He knew he needed to talk to Bas, and it couldn't be on a prison phone.

"A'ight look, give me your number," Santiago instructed. Once Nazir gave it, Santiago continued. "Expect a call from me soon. And all this you tellin' me better be official."

"I'm official, so I don't spit nothing less," Nazir shot back.

"We'll see." Santiago stood up.

"Ay yo, unc, you heard from Tariq? I been tryin' to get at him for a minute," Nazir asked.

"In here."

"In there?" Nazir echoed, brow furled.

"Yeah."

Nazir shook his head. Shit didn't add up. "A'ight."

"Be expectin' my call."

They hung up and went their separate ways. By the time Nazir reached his car, his phone rang. He looked down and didn't recognize the number. He started not to answer, but when he remembered Santiago's words he hit answer.

"Yo."

"This you, Nas?" Cookie asked.

"Yeah."

"Tariq told me to tell you he on the way to my crib. He said meet him here."

At first, Nazir couldn't grasp the situation, but then it hit him. *Shorty a snake too. Fuckin' with them nigguhs from that fake crew*, he thought with a cracked, toothy grin.

"Word? Okay, tell him I'm on my way."

"Okay, I will."

Nazir knew his assumption was on point. Bas was a straight up Judas.

Chapter 37

Extradited

The guards were leading Santiago back to his pod when he saw Mercedes. "Ay yo, sarge! I need to see medical," he said with his mouth, but his eyes said, 'I need to see you.'

She got it instantly. "When I get around to it," she sassed back.

"Why the fuck you gotta be a bitch all the time?" he snapped.

She put her hand on her mace can. "What you say?"

"Bitch, you heard me!"

"I see this nigguh ain't learned his lesson. Take his ass to the hole!"

The two cops cuffed him up, then escorted him back to the negation cell just like he planned.

Four hours later, Mercedes came to the door and unlocked the trap.

"Cuff up." She smirked.

"No, it's next time." He smirked back, reminding her of her earlier words.

She giggled. "Boy, it's cameras. I gotta make it look official. I'ma take 'em off this time."

He stepped to the trap and put his hands out, but when she went to cuff him, he snatched the cuffs and cuffed her left wrist.

"Boy!" she exclaimed, wide-eyed. "The cameras!"

"So keep your hands to your side. Open the door."

She gave him a look, then unlocked the door and stepped in.

"Santiago, take this cuff off!" she demanded, but couldn't help but smile.

"Nope." He chuckled, lifting her arms and placing them around his neck, then pushing her against the wall. "Not 'til I'm finished with you."

"I can't stand your ass," she hissed, squeezing her thighs together and feeling the wetness already.

He leaned in to kiss her, but she bit at his tongue.

"Oh, you wanna bite people, huh? Turn your ass around."

Santiago spun her around facing the wall and placed her cuffed hands up against the it. He spread her legs, then slapped her ass hard and watched it jiggle.

"Shit! Don't do that!" she squealed, heart rate thumping.

Smack!

"Shut up!" he growled in her ear.

"San—"

Smack!

"What I just say?"

Mercede's pussy was on fire, the ass slap just set her on edge. Santiago kissed behind her ear and down to her neck while he took off her belt and let it fall to the floor.

"My pussy throbbin' so hard," she gasped.

He dropped her pants to her ankles and ran a finger down the crack of her ass to her pussy lips. They were so wet her juices instantly slicked his fingers.

"Fuck! What you do to me?" she groaned, arching her back and sticking her ass out.

Santiago squatted behind her and ran his tongue along the same route his finger went, over the crack of her ass and to her pussy. By the time he got to her pussy, she was so wet he could drink from her and he did.

"Oooohhh!" she squealed, the vibration of his sucking driving her up on her tippy toes.

He darted his tongue in and out her pussy while fingering her with two fingers, curling them and her mind around his will at the same time.

"I want you inside me, baby!" she panted.

Santiago dropped his jumper to a pile around his knees and guided himself to her softest place on earth and began to long dick her hard and fast.

Mercedes pressed her face against the wall and threw that pussy at him with all she had, loving the painful pleasure his rock hard dick was giving her.

"Gimme that dick, daddy! Gimme all this dick!" she groaned.

Santiago spread her ass cheeks, pushing himself deeper and making her whole body tremble like she was cold.

"I'ma-I'ma—" she stuttered.

Santiago snatched his dick out, pressing his hard quivering dick against the crack of her ass.

"See how it feel?" he growled deliciously in her ear. "You wanna cum bad, don't you?"

Mercedes nodded vigorously. "Daddy pleasssssse," she pleaded.

"Beg me. Beg me to make you cum," he demanded, toying with her trembling emotions.

"Please make me cum. I'll do whateva you want, just make me cum," she whined.

He slammed his dick back in and took her breath away. "Cum on this dick, you sexy black bitch. Cream all over it," he panted, stroking her hard.

"I–I ahhhh!" she screamed, sounding like she was speaking in tongues. Santiago bit her on the back of her neck, making her pussy walls twitch.

"Tell me I'm the man," he said into her neck.

"You ain't shit." She laughed. "You gonna drive me crazy, you know that?"

Santiago just smiled to himself, but didn't reply. He pulled up his jumper, then her pants and took out her handcuff key to take off the cuffs.

"I need you to answer something for me," he told her.

"What?" she asked, putting her cuffs back in the case on her belt.

"I need a phone."

"I'll have you one tomorrow, unless you need to use mine tonight," Mercedes offered.

"Naw, it needs to be unreachable, so just get a prepaid joint."

"No problem. Anything else?"

He looked at her with a smirk. He could see she was trying to be his ride or die chick, but he just didn't know if she really knew how hard he rode.

"Naw. But you can leave me back here for a few days. I need to think."

"Done. Now"—she began folding her arms over her breasts—"I need something from you."

"You just got it," he quipped playfully.

She hit him on the chest. "Don't play with me, Santiago"

He chuckled. "My bad, ma. What up?"

"Who came to see you today?

"Huh?"

"If you could huh, you could hear," she retorted, snaking her neck. "Now answer the question."

"A young dude from my team, Miss Bossy," he replied.

"Mm-hmm, you know I can find out."

"Ma, believe me. I don't do no lyin' on that tip. If it was a female I'd tell you."

"I was just checkin' to make sure that triflin' bitch you call a wife ain't come, because in here, I'm your wife," she declared with a subtle anxiety to her sass.

Santiago chuckled. "Word? It's like that?" he answered as she started toward the door. "Okay, walk nasty then," he added.

Mercedes turned back to him, slightly flustered.

"Oh! I almost forgot to tell you. They came and got Tariq."

"Who came and got him?"

"Two detectives, a white chick and a black dude."

"For what?" Santiago quizzed.

"They said he's being extradited back to B-more," she answered.

Santiago scowled. The shit didn't taste right, like gumbo without the accent.

"Find out for what and who the detectives were."

"I got you, baby." She winked.

"No doubt."

"No." She stopped and looked him in the eyes. "I don't think you understand. I said I got . . . you."

He smiled because he definitely understood.

"We'll see."

Chapter 38

A Nasty Surprise

I thought you said the nigguh was on his way," the tall goon questioned, glancing at his watch.

He and the second goon, a fat, mini Biggie, were playing Madden on Cookie's Xbox, sitting in the living room.

"That's what he said," she shot back.

"That was an hour ago," he reminded her, impatience coloring his tone.

"You want me to call him again?" she asked, picking up her phone.

"Naw, that'll set that nigguh off on us. Just chill yo, he'll be here," Lil' Biggie surmised.

"I know y'all got somethin' to toot," Cookie said with playful anticipation in her voice.

"Naw yo, we don't sniff that shit," the tall dude replied, then glanced at her with disdain, adding, "or nothing else wit' it either."

Cookie sucked her teeth and rolled her eyes. "Whateva. This nigguh need to come on. I got to go."

"Yeah, you do," the tall goon joked to himself, imagining her head exploding like a melon.

*****

Downstairs in the alley behind Cookie's building, Nazir looked around in the dark, squinting hard for just the right tool.

"There we go," he remarked, spotting an open sardine can with the top peeled back instead of rolled.

He picked up the can, careful not to spill the remaining sardine juice on him. He worked the top back and forth trying to wiggle it loose. He grabbed it wrong and even though it came off, he cut his hand on the edge and spilled the sardine juice on his jeans and Jordans.

"Shit!" he said, looking at his Jordans. "Goddamn!" he hissed, sucking the blood from his palm. "Fuck around and get gangrene behind this shit!"

He tucked the sardine top in his back pocket. Then he jumped up the height of a basketball rim to grab the fire escape ladder with both hands. With one smooth, powerful motion, he pulled himself up, thankful for all those pull-ups he did on the block, waiting for sales to come through. He headed up the fire escape like he knew where he was going because indeed he did.

He knew Tariq had gotten the apartment precisely because the back bedroom window let out on to the fire escape. Combined with the fact that the apartment windows become easier to jimmy after the third floor, and it added up to a very nasty surprise for the two goons.

Nazir got to the window and slid the sardine top between the two sliding window frames, unlocking the window like the swipe of a credit card. Then he slid the window slow . . . and . . .

Squeak!

"Fuck!" he cursed under his breath, hoping that no one heard it.

But Cookie did. She just didn't pay it any mind. She was too focused on getting the monkey off her back.

"Fuck this, I got shit to do. I'm 'bout to call his ass," she huffed, scrolling through her phone.

"Naw yo. Wait—" Lil' Biggie started to say, then he sniffed the air. "Ay yo . . . you smell that?"

"What?" the tall goon asked, eyes glued to the screen.

"Smell like . . . fish . . . sardines," he replied, wrinkling his nose.

"And pork and beans?" Nazir quipped, suddenly appearing from the hallway. Before either man could react, Nazir put a bullet between the tall goon's eyes that had him looking like a red dot Indian. He slumped over on his partner.

Cookie screamed and jumped up.

Nazir shot her in the leg and she began hyperventilating from the agonizing pain, rolling bloody on the carpet.

Lil' Biggie wanted to reach, but he saw it was futile since he was staring cockeyed at the barrel of Nazir's gun, it was so close.

"You—you got it, Nas. You got it," he stammered.

Nazir shook his head with a wicked smirk. "Word up, Tee, like that? You was gonna murder me, son?"

"Yo fam', my word."

Nas hawked spit in his face. The green gook ran down his cheek. "Don't call me fam', call me sir. You wanna treat me like a stranger, address me as one," Nas seethed.

"Ye–ye–yes sir."

"Pull out your phone. Call Bas. Tell him y'all fucked up and I got away."

"Huh?"

"Huh what?"

Smack!

"Huh, sir, huh, sir!"

"Take out your phone, slow."

Lil' Biggie did as he was told.

"Dial the number."

With shaking hands, he scrolled to Bas's number, then hit send.

"Yo," Bas answered with anticipation.

"It's him," Lil Biggie said to Nas.

"It?" Bas said.

"Tell him 'we fucked up. He got away,'" Nas reminded Lil' Biggie.

"We—we fucked up. He got away!"

"What!" Bas barked so loud, Nazir heard it.

He snatched the phone.

"Yeah, yo. I'm on my Scarface shit tonight," Nazir quipped, keeping the gun directly on Lil' Biggie's nose.

Bas was silent for a minute, then replied, "You know this was just business, right nephew?"

Nazir chuckled coldly. "You let them Roach ass nigguhs get to you, huh? What, they sucked your dick? They let you suck theirs?"

Bas snorted. "I'll see you soon, nephew."

"Fo' sho, unc." Nazir hung up and tossed the phone aside, then looked at Lil' Biggie.

"You wanna look like Biggie for real?"

"Huh?"

Boc! Boc!

Nazir pumped two in his face, the first blowing his eyeball from the socket, and the second, exploded his brains out the side of his head.

"Now, I meant after death," Nazir sneered, then squatted down behind Cookie.

She could hardly catch her breath.

"Breathe, ma, breathe."

"Please! Please!" she screamed hoarsely.

He snatched her up by her hair, pulling her up as she tried to balance on one leg.

"I always told Tariq not to trust you . . . too bad I was right."

"I—" was all she got out.

He grabbed her up and tossed her face first through the window. Her body fell on a jagged piece of glass at the base of the window as the momentum flipped her out and over, eight flights, landing with a sickening crack of her neck.

"It's always the one closest to you," Nazir mumbled as he headed out the way he came.

Chapter 39

Battle Raging Within

I want to see my daddy."

Nina laughed. "You sound like you scared of the dark. You want a teddy bear, too?"

"Fuck you!" Eva gritted. "I want to see my daddy."

"Fuck you! We ain't got no daddy. We all we got." Nina could feel Eva seething inside.

"Let. Me. Out!" Eva barked.

"You said you wanted to be dead, remember? Be dead."

"Not so you could live!"

Nina laughed out loud, then said, "Don't lie. You like when I'm in control, don't you? You know why? Because I'm a bad bitch and you're just . . . you."

"Eva, who are talking to?"

Nina, standing in the open refrigerator door, looked over her shoulder at Mel, giving her an up and down gaze. Then she spat with disdain, "Nobody."

Mel slammed the refrigerator, just missing Nina's face. She glared at Mel, who stepped right in her face.

"Bitch, I wish you would," Eva hissed coldly.

"You think I don't see what you're doing? Stay. Away. From. Bas," Mel threatened.

Nina laughed and covered her mouth with her hand. "Really? Wow . . . I guess I was the one raping him on the couch while his mother watched."

Mel smirked coldly. "Bitch, you deserve it. You wanna be pretty? You wanna be trusting? Then that's what pretty and trusting get you in this world," Mel hissed.

"Whateva!" Nina spat, then started to turn away.

"I want you out of my house today."

Nina stopped and turned back to Mel. She gave her a once over like a common bitch in the street.

"What's the matter? Can't handle the competition, mother?" Nina retorted, and the way she curled the "M," there was no doubt in Mel's mind that Eva was really saying fuck her.

Mel hauled off and slapped Nina so hard, she turned her whole torso. Nina recovered and went behind her back and came out with a snub nose .38 so quick, Mel didn't see it until the steel kissed her upper lip like mwah!

"Go 'head . . . slap me again. I dare you. . . No, I beg you. Please!" Nina seethed.

The look in Nina's eyes froze Mel. *This . . . is not my daughter*, was all she could think.

For a moment, Nina stared at her unblinking. Then she shrugged, cocked the hammer, and hissed, "Fuck it."

Simultaneously, Mel on the outside and Eva on the inside screamed, "Noooooooo!"

Nina strained to pull the trigger, but her finger wouldn't budge. "Let go of me!" she gritted.

"No! You ain't killin' my mother!" Eva bassed firmly.

Never had Nina felt Eva's strength. She was powerless to do anything.

Mel stood rooted to the spot and had no idea of the battle raging within her daughter.

"Eva . . . please . . . I–I love you," Mel whispered.

"Lyin' bitch!" Nina barked, wanting with everything to squeeze the trigger.

Everything, except Eva.

"No," was all Eva said, calmly and evenly.

Nina's shoulders relaxed, and a smile spread across her face. "You lucky she loves you, too," she replied and turned away.

Stunned, Mel stood there and watched her daughter walk out. She didn't know what just happened, but whatever it was, it left her wet . . .

From the pee puddle at her feet.

Chapter 40

A Perfectly Executed Setup

A chair . . . is still a chair, even when there's no one sitting there . . ." Luther wooed in the background while Mel sat on Bas's dick and rode him slow and hard, her hands gripping his chest as he pushed so deep, she could feel it in her stomach.

"Oh, Bas, don't stop! Don't ever stop," she gasped, trying to forget about the earlier incident with Eva.

"Tell me you love me," Bas commanded.

"Oh, I doooo. I love you, I love you," she groaned.

His phone rang. He reached for it.

Mel grabbed his hand. "Baby, no, I'm so close," she whined.

"I have to, ma. Shit is hectic in them streets," he explained, because he knew having Nazir on the loose meant he was now exposed because of it.

He answered, thinking it was one of his goons. "Speak."

"It's me."

Bas's hips stopped grinding, and he could hardly hear over his own pounding heartbeat. "Santiago?" he said, barely able to hide the surprise in his voice.

When Mel heard who it was, her pussy twitched and got even wetter knowing she was fucking Bas while her no-good husband was on the other end. She threw her head back and sped up her pace.

"Yessss!" she gushed.

Bas put his finger to her mouth to silence her, but she put it in her mouth and began sucking on it.

"You sound surprised," Santiago said.

"Naw, naw, I ain't expect—you out?" Bas questioned.

"Naw, they still ain't give me a bond."

Bas relaxed with relief, but replied, "Damn, fam'. What you need me to do?"

"Come see me."

Mel began bouncing on his dick, her eyes rolling up in the back of her head.

Bas grunted.

"Bas, you okay?"

"Yeah, yeah, I'm good. When you want me to come—I mean—be there?"

"Tomorrow."

There was an element of edge in Santiago's response, one that made Bas feel a need to be cautious. His plan wasn't fully completed, so he couldn't just blow Santiago off. Still, he wasn't going to go see him because he didn't want Santiago to know his whereabouts so easily.

"No doubt. I'll be there," he lied.

"And Bas . . . I need you to go by my house. And check on things. I've been trying to call Eva but she ain't answerin'. Check on her and Mel for me."

Bas couldn't suppress a smile, knowing he was already in his house and in his pussy with Mel cumming all over his dick at that moment.

"I'll handle it." He smirked, gripping Mel's hip.

They hung up.

Mel bent over and sucked his bottom lip.

"He told you to check on me, didn't he?" She leered, knowing her husband well. They laughed. Her phone rang. They looked at each other knowingly.

"You gonna answer?" he asked, wearing a grin as Luther crooned on.

"Why not?"

*****

Santiago paced the cell as he waited for Mel to answer. A knot began forming in his stomach. She answered. It unballed and fluttered.

"Hello?" she said, dead pan.

"Mel."

"What?" she answered coldly.

Bas couldn't resist the opportunity. He pinched her clit, and she had to fight back a moan.

"How you doin'?"

"What do you"—her pussy twitched, filled with Bas's dick—"want."

"You okay?"

"No. I was sleep."

Santiago sighed. He could hear the wall that had been erected between them in her every word. He knew he was the cause of that wall, but he also wanted to be the cause of it falling.

"Listen, ma . . . I know shit is fucked up between us . . . I fucked it up. I expect that. But I do love you and I promise you, whatever it takes, I'm willing to do to make it right, okay?"

Mel was deep in a down stroke, licking her lips to a deliciousness of the sensation inside, oblivious to Santiago's words.

"Mel? You there?"

Almost, she thought wickedly but said, "Huh?"

"You heard what I said?"

"No, I told you I'm . . . sleep."

Santiago's golden brown hue flushed red. He had poured his heart out, and she hadn't even cared enough to listen.

"Yeah a'ight. I'ma—" he began to say, but then he heard it.

"Pret-ty lit-tle . . . darling have a heart . . . Don't let one mistake keep us apart . . ."

Luther filtered out of the background and filled his consciousness, providing the final piece of the puzzle. If he was red before, he was a volcanic crimson then, but somehow he managed to hold it in.

"Well, if you ain't gonna say nothing—" Mel started to say, but Santiago beat her to the punch.

Click!

It all came rushing in out of a vortex of sounds and images, swirling, mixing, and combining like molecules to form the matter right before his eyes. It all played out almost step by step in reverse, like someone rewinding the tape of his life for the last few months and ended with the words, "I think Mel and Alex are having an affair." It had all been a setup . . . a perfectly executed setup. Bas had played on his sense of guilt impeccably, bringing to life his worst nightmare: Mel's infidelity. And Mel had played her role to a tee, making him think she was having an affair with Alex when it was really with Bas. The truth gives a lie wings . . .

Alex . . . Santiago's stomach cringed.

He had been fooled just as much as Santiago had. It really had been a surprise party, or so he thought. So the smile at the door wasn't to challenge him, it was merely to welcome him. Alex loved Santiago like a brother, even though he knew he had murdered his father.

Like father like son.

Santiago sat down on the bunk with his head in his hands. All he could see were Mel and Bas doing exactly what they were doing at the moment. Fucking. But instead of screams of passion, there was mocking laughter. The sound filled his head, then filled the cell, echoing off the steel and concrete. He pictured himself tied up and gagged, watching Bas fuck his wife and there was nothing he could do about it.

The rage bubbled up from his gut and he vomited, expelling a deep guttural grunt. He wanted to smash, destroy, crush, kill and then . . .

Laugh.

It started as a little chuckle, then erupted into a rumbling cackle. It took the place of tears.

"They played the shit outta me!" He laughed.

But the laughing cleared his mind, and it was like a veil was lifted. Everything became clear. And just as quickly as it started, the laughter ended.

He snatched the phone off the bed, then tried to uplink to the Internet. He paced the floor staring at the little screen as it tried to find a strong enough signal to connect. When it did, he quickly went to Google and typed in:

`Vito Colon`

The screen blinked, then came back with several Vitos. It wasn't until he got to the last that he knew why something told him to do it.

Two men found dead in their home.

One Vito Colon 78, and Manuel Ortego were found shot to death in . . .

Santiago slapped the flip phone shut. He had read enough to know everything. Not only was Bas betraying him, he was doing it with the Rosario Brothers. Now, his rage turned to cold calculation. He knew what he had to do.

Santiago flipped open the phone, then dialed Nazir's number from memory. After five rings it went to voice mail. Santiago figured he didn't answer because he didn't know the number, and he smiled to himself. He liked the young boy. He could see his future in his eyes.

He texted: *It's Santiago. Pick up.*

Once the text was sent, he didn't even have a chance to dial before Nazir was calling him.

"I told you to be on the lookout for my call," Santiago reminded him as soon as he answered.

"I was. I just ain't know the number."

"Then you shoulda picked up."

"I decided to call instead," Nazir shot back, and Santiago couldn't help but grin at his sharpness. His next words made the smile drop from his face.

"You were right," Santiago admitted.

A moment of silence.

"So what do we do now?" was all Nazir wanted to know.

"We?" Santiago smirked.

"I fuck with your son hard body, and I work for you. That's the basis of the we. I'm already committed," he vowed.

"Naw yo, you used to work for me," Santiago replied.

Heavy silence, then Santiago added, "Now you work with me."

He could hear the relief in Nazir's chuckle. "Don't fuck wit' a nigguh head like that, unc. I ain't took my meds in like a week," Nazir joked.

Santiago laughed.

"Yous a funny nigguh, Nas. But check it . . . this is what we gonna do . . ."

Chapter 41

This Ain't About Feelings

Tariq stared at the yellow tape on the side of the building and across his apartment's broken window. The only person around was an old scraggly wino.

"Ay yo, you know what happened?" Tariq asked.

"Do I know? Man, I was right here. I'm talkin' about right here when it went down! I heard like a hun-ned shots," he said, exaggerating the story for effect. "And I realized they were coming from up there somewhere. So I looked up and pssssss! Bitch come out of the window, head first and come straight down! Landed on her neck like the bitch was tryin' to breakdance!"

Tariq unconsciously balled his fists at his sides. It wasn't so much the fact that Cookie was dead, but why he thought she had died. He started to walk away.

"Hold up, I ain't tell you about the two dead muhfuckas in the apartment."

Tariq ignored him and got in his car. He couldn't believe Santiago had had Cookie killed. For him, there was no other explanation in his crack-ravaged mind. He thought Santiago did it as a prelude to what was next. Tariq's death.

He grabbed the crack pipe off the passenger seat and packed it with a chunk of rock. He didn't care who saw him blast off in broad daylight behind the wheel of his car. He needed to get his head together.

Sssssssss.

The sizzle of the smoldering rock crackled through the car and wreaked havoc with his every sense. Exhaling, he felt like soothing harps were playing in his head.

His phone rang. Tariq knew who it was. He answered.

"Yeah."

"Welcome back. Didn't I tell you I'd take care of you?" Melissa remarked.

"Yeah . . . you did."

"The official story is you were extradited back to Baltimore, then given more bond, so you're in the clear.

"He killed her," he stated, rubbing his temples.

"I'm a homicide detective, Tariq. You're going to have to be more specific about that," Melissa replied.

"Cookie. The chick I got popped with in B-more. Santiago had her fuckin' killed!" Tariq gritted.

"With all due respect, Tariq, that's irrelevant to the bigger picture. Just add it to your reasons why you know we have to work together, okay?" she said.

"Yeah, yo."

"Now, I've got some people who want to meet you. How quickly can you get to the north side?"

"Where at?"

"Just call me when you get there."

"I'm on my way."

She told Tariq to meet her in the back of a restaurant. Within the hour, he was parking in the alley where the restaurant's loading dock for deliveries were. He got out of the car as Melissa approached.

"Maybe you should eat something while you're here. You look like shit," she commented.

"Fuck you!" Tariq spat.

She shrugged. "Turn around. I have to frisk you."

He put his hands on the roof of his car. She ran her hands in and out, all over his body expertly. When she ran her hand along his thigh and felt his dick, she gave it a little squeeze, saying, "I may just have to take you up on that earlier offer."

"I know that's right." Tariq chuckled.

The two of them walked inside, oblivious to the fact that they were being watched from down by the block through a pair of binoculars. It was Melissa's partner, Detective James Lawrence.

Inside, Melissa led Tariq into the back office of the restaurant. He started to walk in, until he saw who sat behind the desk.

Chez Rosario.

"Fuck no! Fuckin' hell no! What kind of shit is you into? I thought you were a cop!" Tariq shot accusingly at Melissa.

Regardless of the situation, the Rosarios were still the roaches in his book.

"Nephew, relax. You haven't even heard what the man has to say."

Tariq heard the voice, but he couldn't believe it until he turned his head and saw Bas sitting just to the right of the door.

"Uncle Bas? What the hell are you doin' here?" Tariq exclaimed.

Bas stood up and looked at Chez.

"Ay, Chez, you mind if I have a private word with my nephew?" Bas requested.

"By all means," Chez replied with an amused expression.

Bas turned to Tariq. "Come on, neph. Let me holla at you."

Tariq followed him into the next room, a small stock room filled with canned goods. Bas closed the door.

"Look, I know this shit look crazy, but let me bring you up to speed. Matter of fact, naw . . . let me take you back," Bas remarked.

"What you mean?" Tariq asked.

"When you were younger . . . you remember your great uncle, Carlos?"

Tariq smiled. "No doubt. I used to call him granddaddy because I didn't have one."

Bas nodded grimly. "I know this is gonna fuck you up, but . . . your father had him killed." Bas left out the part that he set up the hit.

"What?" Tariq's eyes bulged.

"Yeah, yo . . . your father is . . . how can I say it . . . for years, I've loved Santiago as a brother and I still do, but he ain't right, yo. He'll eat his own just to be on top. He also killed Alex with his own hands."

Tariq shook his head. Bas had just confirmed what Tariq had seen in Santiago's eyes.

"I . . . I know."

"You do?"

Tariq nodded.

"Confronted him in the county. He ain't deny it."

Bas put his hand on Tariq's shoulders. "It's no doubt in my mind that sooner or later I'd be next. I wasn't about to let that happen. And Tariq . . . he knows about your addiction, so you know what that means."

Tariq fought to hold back the tears. Bas's head game was working perfectly.

"Now listen to me," Bas began, looking in his eyes. "This shit ain't about feelings. It's about business. Chez is a businessman. Are you?"

"No doubt," Tariq confirmed.

Bas smiled. "Then we can do business. Bottom line, if what he talkin' is good, then we roll wit' it, all right? You wit' me?" Bas questioned, holding out his hand.

Tariq smiled and shook it. "You already know, unc."

"Let's go do business then."

Chapter 42

Wicked Intentions

Thank you for letting me stay with you," Nina remarked sweetly.

"Of course, yo, you're my girl," Asia chirped, plastic smile firmly in place.

"No, you are my girl. Look at you, you are so pretty," Nina snickered.

They were sitting on Asia's bed, listening to music.

"Thank you," Asia beamed.

Nina ran her hand through Asia's long hair. It was almost as long as her own.

"You know what? You'll look real cute with a short cut. Like a pixie cut, spiked up though," Nina envisioned.

"Ain't no way! I love my hair. I would never get it cut," Asia replied, smiling.

"That wasn't a suggestion, silly," Nina answered, her voice syrupy sweet, but her eyes stone cold.

Asia just looked at her. "Eva, I—"

"Who?"

"I meant Nina, I don't want to cut my hair," Asia protested weakly.

"Don't worry, it's going to look real cute . . . we should dye it red. No, that's so common. Pink! No, too pony . . . I know . . . sky blue!" Nina clapped excitedly, like she had found the cure for cancer.

All Asia could think was how she could get away from this crazy bitch, but she knew, as long as Nina had that gun with her fingerprints on it, she was stuck.

"Yeah, sky blue. You're so cute, just like a little baby doll. You want to be my baby doll?"

Asia nodded, like a wooden doll.

Nina smiled brightly. "I thought you would. Now . . . take off my shoes," Nina instructed her, holding up her right Air Max.

"Ev—I mean—Nina. I swear I would've never did it if Tariq hadn't gotten me involved. I didn't know what to do. I was so scared." Asia teared up.

"Shhhh, doll babies don't cry. Take off my shoe."

Asia gripped the shoe, toe and heel, then pulled it off.

"Now, the other one," Nina sang, her voice light and fluffy.

Asia took off the left shoe.

"My feet don't stink, do they?" Nina asked, putting her socked foot in Asia's face. Asia couldn't speak because she was choked with tears, so she simply shook her head.

"Good. Now . . . take off my pants," Nina instructed her, her full smile now completely gone.

Asia looked at Nina, because she could see her wicked intentions in her eyes. She couldn't hold it back any more, as tears burst from her eyes.

"No. Please, Nina, don't make me do this. I'm so . . . sorry!"

"Shhhhhh . . . show me." Nina smirked.

Asia slowly climbed on the bed on shaky knees and reached for Nina's button. She undid it with shaking hands, then looped her fingers over her pants' top, to pull them down, careful not to include her panties. Nina grabbed her wrist, then without taking her eyes off Asia, looped Asia's thumbs inside her panties. Asia pulled down her pants and panties, as Nina lifted her hips so she could pull them over her ample ass.

"Smell that? That's my happy place," Nina whispered, caressing Asia's cheeks. Nina spread her legs, pressing the heels of her feet into the bed for leverage, then pressed Asia's head down to her pussy.

"Now . . . lick my pussy," Nina commanded.

Asia stuck out her tongue and closed her eyes, then licked up the length of Nina's pussy.

Nina let out a slight whimper and squirmed, but remarked, "Don't tease me. Lick it like you like your pussy to be licked."

Nina gripped both sides of her head and guided her like a human vibrator to the places she desired most. Nina fucked her face, grinding into her and soaking her chin and cheeks. She lifted her leg high, cocking it back and guided Asia's tongue to her asshole.

"Stick your tongue in it," Nina cooed, licking her lips.

Asia felt so humiliated, so violated. Her passive anger boiled inside her, making her tears slide down the sides of her face. Nina worked her head back and forth, making Asia's tongue go in and out her asshole.

"Oh fuck, Asia! You're gonna make me come! Don't stop!" she urged, as if she wasn't just using Asia to do it to herself.

Nina's pussy exploded, drenching her thighs and the bed beneath her. She guided Asia's face back to her pussy.

"Lick it up, lick it all up," Nina moaned.

Asia was numb. Nina had basically raped her and that's how she felt. Feeling Nina's thick cum go down her throat, she sobbed hard and long. Nina hugged her to her pelvis.

"That's it, baby, let it out. You'll get used to it," Nina said.

Nina's phone rang. She felt so relaxed, so in control, even though she didn't know the number, she answered anyway.

"Baby girl!"

The sound of Santiago's deep, strong voice caught her off guard. She hadn't expected it. Every time his number came up, she would send it to voice mail because she knew, if Eva heard that voice . . .

"Daddy! Oh my God, I miss you so much!" Eva exclaimed, emerging from within like someone submerged under water.

Hearing the joy in his baby girl's voice made Santiago instantly tear up. He had missed her so much, and now that he decided on what his next move was, speaking to her was that much more important. But what he heard next, he totally didn't expect. It sounded like the exorcist on the other line when he heard his daughter say, "What the fuck are you callin' for? We don't need you, motherfucka! I hope you fuckin' rot in there, you weak piece of shit!"

Santiago couldn't believe his ears. He didn't know what to say, each word feeling like a razor blade giving his heart multiple buck–fifties.

"Ev—" he started to say, but the line went dead in his hands.

"Aarrrgggh!" Nina screamed as she launched her phone against the wall and watched it explode in a thousand pieces.

Asia watched in horror. She looked at Nina, chest heaving.

"Eva . . . what is wrong with you?"

No sooner did she get the words out of her mouth, than she found herself pinned up against the wall, being choked with two hands.

"What did I tell you my name is, bitch?" Nina seethed, her face inches from Asia's.

"Ni–Ni–Nina," Asia choked, clawing at Nina's hands.

"Nina, bitch! Not Eva. Nina! Don't fuckin' try to play with me because I know what you're doing!"

Nina let her go, and Asia slumped against the wall, wheezing and gasping for air. Nina stood over her, glaring. "Go run my bath water. Now!"

Asia rolled off the wall and stumbled into the bathroom.

Nina began to pace the floor like a female Santiago. The one thing she couldn't stand was not being in control. It was her weakness and it scared her. Inside, she could hear Eva laughing, mocking, because now she knew her weakness, too.

"Soon," Eva whispered.

"Bitch, you wish," Nina spat.

Now that she was in the driver's seat, she wasn't about to let go. She'd kill herself and Eva too before she did that.

While Nina paced, Asia brushed her teeth. Hard. She scrubbed her tongue with her toothbrush until her tongue felt raw, but she still couldn't get Nina's taste off her tongue. She looked at herself in the mirror as she brushed, thinking about what she had just witnessed.

Asia knew about split personalities. She studied psychology books, hoping to one day become a shrink once she graduated college. She now understood why Eva was acting so different, wanting to be known by another name and the whole nine.

"... I'm having crazy dreams yo, like ... crazy. It's like, it feels like me but it's not me, you know?" Asia remembered Eva saying.

Asia understood perfectly. She heard the way Nina responded to Santiago. That was all Eva. Asia knew that Eva was her only hope. Eva wouldn't treat her like this. Eva would understand. Eva would forgive her. Asia knew, the only way to save herself ... was to save Eva.

Chapter 43

Suicide

Santiago wrapped his bed sheet and then knotted it around his neck. He was standing on the steel sink in his cell. The other end of the sheet was tied to the light fixture on the ceiling. He had thought about writing a suicide note, but he figured his swinging body would speak for itself. He yanked on the sheet once more to make sure the fixture was strong enough to hold his weight.

"Hey! What are you doing in here?" the officer cried out, fumbling with his keys.

Santiago stepped off the sink.

"Nooo!" the officer bellowed, grabbing his walkie-talkie. "D-wing! D-wing! Code 5 suicide attempt!"

He dropped the keys, but snatched them up, and stuck the proper one in the lock. When he rushed in, Santiago was twitching and kicking. The officer grabbed his leg and pulled. Santiago gagged. Realizing he couldn't pull him down, he lifted his body to take the pressure off.

"Just hold on!" the officer urged.

Several seconds later, several officers rushed in being led by Mercedes.

"Oh my God! Cut him down! Cut him down!" she screamed, grabbing her walkie-talkie. "We need the ambulance ripped and ready to go ASAP! We've got a suicide attempt!" she turned to two officers. "You two, go get strapped. You'll be the tail car! Go!"

The officers nodded and ran out. By the time she turned around, they had Santiago lying on the floor.

"Is he . . . dead?" she asked.

"No, no, but his pulse feels weak."

"Okay, stay with him. I'm going to strap up!" Mercedes barked as she ran out the door.

They kept an ambulance by the back dock of the jail because so many violent fights broke out. So the ambulance was ready in seconds. The two EMS workers on duty wheeled Santiago out on the stretcher. Mercedes and the officer that originally found Santiago jumped in the back with him. Behind them were two heavily armed officers in the escort car. The wail of the ambulance siren set the rhythm as it screeched off.

As they zoomed along the city streets, the officer looked down at Santiago's closed eyes and remarked,

"Didn't look much like a kingpin hanging from that rope."

"I'm sure he didn't," Mercedes replied sourly.

The officer started to say something, but a quick metallic flash shooting by the window caught his eye.

"What the—shit?"

At the same time, the two escort officers were joking about the same thing.

"Shit . . . all the time he facing, I woulda tried to kill myself too!" The driver laughed.

The passenger turned to comment, but he saw what the officer in the ambulance thought was a metallic flash.

It was a silver Silverado truck coming, barreling off the side street.

"Look out!" the passenger cried, but it was too late.

The Silverado, timing the intersection and acceleration like a true car thief, shot out of the side street, running the red light and ramming directly into the side of the escort vehicle. They were hit so hard, the driver was knocked unconscious and would later die of blunt force trauma. The passenger was dead.

And then everything seemed to go in slow motion . . .

Santiago had planned it all to a science. He knew the jail's policy on suicide because Mercedes had told him.

"They have to take you to an outside hospital," she informed him.

"Have to?"

"Have to."

He just smiled.

Then he waited for the officer to do his rounds, which was every fifteen minutes. As soon as he said, "Hey!" Santiago stepped off the sink.

Finally, he had Nazir to handle the streets.

"Only nigguhs you can absolutely trust," Santiago had emphasized.

"Zoo Crew," Nazir replied, like it was the most obvious thing in the world.

"Zoo Crew?" Santiago echoed.

"That's my crew of goons, strictly official tissue, unc. Don't worry, they can handle it," Nazir assured him.

"They better."

And they did.

As soon as Santiago heard the loud crunch of the crash, slow motion kicked into overdrive as Santiago jumped up from the stretcher, grabbed Mercedes's gun out of her holster, and aimed at the other officer. He turned his attention back to Santiago just in time to see that death was coming.

Boc! Boc! Boc!

All three were head shots since he was wearing a vest. He pointed the gun at Mercedes.

"Get down!"

She screamed and complied just like they talked about. He aimed the gun at the EMS workers.

"Stop this motherfucka now! And get out!"

Screech!

It came to a complete stop. They got out and jetted.

He aimed the gun back at Mercedes and smiled.

"I wish I could go with you," she remarked.

"Ma, we talked about this. I need you here to throw 'em off the scent. We'll meet up later," he promised.

"Damn skippy we will," she sassed, laughing.

"You ready?"

She nodded, her face turning pale. He bent and kissed her lips.

"I love you."

Boc!

The shot went through the fleshy part of her thigh. She screamed out, "Fuck!"

"You okay?"

She glowered at him like he had two heads. "Hell no! You just shot me! And Santiago, I know you don't love me, but thank you for saying it. It took the sting out."

He smiled and kissed her. "I gotta go," he replied, then hopped out the ambulance.

"But you will . . . you will," she mumbled to herself.

Nazir skidded up in a stolen whip, the trunk already popped. He had hardly stopped, before Santiago open the trunk then lay inside and closed the trunk. Nazir skidded off, fleeing the scene clean.

Chapter 44

A Slow, Malicious Smile

oosh! Was the sound of Bas dropping the bottle of brandy he had in his hand when he heard the news. Mel had called him on the phone crying.

"Ma, what's wrong? Calm down, I can't understand you!" he said, trying to understand her ramblings.

"Santiago . . . is out! He's out! He broke out of jail!" she screamed.

That's when Bas dropped the bottle.

She had been watching *The Young and the Restless*, when they interrupted with a special news bulletin. She saw the ambulance in the middle of the street surrounded by police. Then they flashed his picture on the screen, and he seemed to be looking at her.

Bas couldn't believe his ears.

He didn't think Santiago had put two and two together, but he definitely wasn't about to take chances.

"Okay . . . don't worry, but we gonna handle this, a'ight? We just probably need to fall back for a second," he suggested.

Mel knew she was being thrown under the bus, but she knew the feeling well enough to take it in stride. "Whateva!" she tossed back at him, then hung up.

Bas could tell she was mad, but she'd get over it. He knew it wasn't only the strong that survived. The weak survived by hiding.

*****

"He'll come for me," Eva remarked with grateful certainty.

Nina smirked. "Over our dead body."

"You wouldn't?"

"Didn't you?" Nina stared at the same TV news scene that Mel had seen.

"Three officers were killed. Two were killed in the accident and one by a gunshot wound believed to have been issued by Acevedo. A fourth officer was also shot, but is expected to survive," the reporter said.

Nina couldn't help but be impressed when the reporter explained how he made his escape.

"I see where I get it from," she said.

"He's coming," Eva taunted.

"So am I," Nina replied, because she knew, the only way to beat the hunter, is to make him the hunted.

*****

Santiago had Nazir and Kika in stitches. They were in a loft apartment Santiago kept in the cut that no one knew about.

"And the motherfucka fumbling with the goddamn keys! I'm danglin' for real, cussing this nigguh out like: nigguh hurry your ass up!"

They howled.

"So I'm steppin' back on the sink when he ain't tryin' to take the pressure off! So he ran in and guess what this goddamn nigguh do!"

"What?" Nazir asked.

"This motherfucka grabbed my legs and pulled! I'm like you goddamn dummy, you killin' me! I'm chokin' like a muhfucka!" Santiago laughed.

Kika shook her head.

"You too much, Mr. Acevedo. But do you have to use the Lord's name in vain so much?"

"She's a Jesus freak," Nazir quipped.

Kika mushed him. "I ain't no kind of freak, nigguh!"

"My bad, my bad." Nazir chuckled.

He could tell Kika was feeling Santiago. At first, she didn't like the fact that they were going to be staying with a fugitive. But the objection seemed to end as soon as she laid eyes on him.

Santiago smiled. "I told you, ma, call me Santiago. And you're right. I'll be more careful."

The smile he flashed her made it impossible for Kika to hide the blush.

"So what now, unc?" Nazir asked.

Santiago leaned back in the armchair and crossed his legs, right over left. "We lay low. Let the streets digest this. Let 'em choose sides, feel me? Now, I'm not gonna be able to move at all. You gonna have to be my arms and legs. Can you handle that?"

Nazir was taken aback by the question. He knew Santiago was putting a lot on his shoulders. Without hesitation, he replied, "No doubt."

Santiago nodded.

"Good. And like I said, make sure our people are solid. Your Zoo Crew came through today. Tell the dude drivin', he timed that shit beautifully."

"It wasn't a dude. That was Shamekka. Wait till you meet her." He shook his head.

"No doubt . . . believe me, Nas, we about to put an end to this Rosario shit, once and for all," Santiago vowed, and the coldness in his eyes sent a delicious chill through Kika.

"What about Bas?" Nazir questioned.

A slow, malicious smile spread across Santiago's face.

Tasha Macklin

"I'll take care of Bas . . . personally."

Chapter 45

Business with Pleasure

The music was banging and the atmosphere was lush, sexy, and decadent in Antonio's lounge, Cherry. He had it modeled similar to the 40/40 club, and it was one of the hottest spots in the city.

He sat down, status surveying the layout. He had won. Tariq could not keep up with his swag. Antonio was the young boss extraordinaire, and he wanted the whole game to bow down.

But as he sat back in his booth surrounded by yes men, bodyguards, and bad bitches, he saw someone coming through the crowd that made his dick twitch in his pants.

Not only him, but it seemed every dude in the club stopped just to watch Nina come through. Dressed in a sleek, black bodycon dress with killer Christian Louboutin pumps, the words fierce and sexy announced her entrance. Nothing about her inferred her seventeen years of age. But more than the look, it was simply her presence that made the men pause. Her strut alone made a couple of nigguhs want to masturbate just watching her walk.

Antonio watched her approach with an assured expression. He had always found her sexy, and now, by the look in her eyes, he could tell he was about to get a taste.

She stepped up to the full booth, glanced around, then remarked, "I want to sit down. I want to sit right there!" She pointed at the spot right next to Antonio, the one currently being occupied by a shapely red bone.

Without hesitation, Antonio turned to the red bone. "Beat it."

She sucked her teeth, but didn't hesitate to comply. When the booth was clear, Nina slid in next to Antonio, crossing her legs so that her right leg crossed his as well.

"Damn, Lil' Eva done grew up, huh?" Antonio remarked, looking her up and down.

She giggled then replied, "Would it be wrong if I came to mix business with pleasure?"

"It depends on the business."

"I'm going help you do what you could never do without me."

Antonio looked at her.

"Which is?"

She got close to his ear, nibbled on the lobe, then replied, "Kill Santiago."

THE END

READING GROUP
DISCUSSION QUESTIONS

1.   The book opens with the statement, "I think Mel and Alex are having an affair." If this statement were spoken by your close friend regarding your significant other, how would you handle this situation? Explain in detail.

2.   Did Santiago deserve the treatment he received from his wife Melanie? Bas? Please explain.

3.   Young boys are always looking for role models. Did the three boys, Santiago, Alex, and Basim peeping on Carlos with the beautiful young woman affect them positively or negatively? Please explain.

4.   Childhood experiences sometimes are a determining factor of the mindset a child will later develop as an adult. Did Mel's relationship with Ms. Brooks as well as her relationship with Santiago turn her into the type of person she'd become? Please explain.

5.   Who were your favorite characters? Why?

6.   Should Angel have told Eva or Tariq about Detective Mulligan? Why or why not?

7.   What are your thoughts on the character Eva? Did you feel that because of the drama with her parents, that she somehow was neglected? Explain.

8.   According to WebMD, dissociative identity disorder (multiple personality disorder) is characterized by the

presence of two or more distinct or split identities or personality states that continually have power over the person's behavior. What do you believe caused this disorder to surface in the character Eva? Explain.

9.   Are you convinced that deep down Santiago and Mel loved one another?

10.   Did weakness or fear stop Tariq from living up to his father's expectations? Explain.

11.   How much do you trust your best friend? Would you ever confront a situation based only on the word of your best friend? Explain.

12.   Is there any character that you wanted killed off early? Who? Why?

13.   Had Santiago's quest for power blinded him? Explain. In your view, what kind of person should be given authority over others?

14.   If this book were featured on the big screen, which actors would you choose to play each role?

15.   Besides the theme of power and money, what other themes were prevalent in the book?

16.   Did any part of the book make you uncomfortable? Why?

17.   What was the most important message in the book?

18.   Did any passage stand out to you? Did you learn something you never knew before?

19.   If you could change something about the book, what would it be? Why?

20.   What do you want to see happen in Part 2?

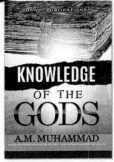

CPSIA information can be obtained
at www.ICGtesting.com
Printed in the USA
LVOW01s1207260916

506233LV00002B/39/P

9 781936 649334